T0194916

Emperors of Salvation

A novel

Malthouse African Fiction

Emperors of Salvation

Hope Eghagha

malthouse

Malthouse Press Limited

Lagos, Benin, Ibadan, Jos, Port-Harcourt, Zaria

Malthouse Press Limited
43 Onitana Street, Off Stadium Hotel Road,
Surulere, Lagos, Lagos State
E-mail: malthouse_press@yahoo.com
malthouselagos@gmail.com
Tel: +234 (01) -773 53 44; 0802 600 3203

First Published 2009
ISBN 978 978 8422 06 8

Distributors:
African Books Collective
Oxford, United Kingdom
Email: abc@africanbookscollective.com
Website: http://www.africanbookscollective.com

The daylight may always come, but it does not come
for everybody and does not come on time.

- James Baldwin.

Let the prophet speak. Let the mad man speak.
The man whose words come to pass
Is our true son, our true prophet.

- hope eghagha

How long shall they kill our prophets
while we stand aside and look?

-- Bob Marley.

February 19....

Dear Bojor Aruedon,
It is not only the pain that our hands cannot reach the fruits of the tree planted in our garden and in our farms that torments us. Sometimes, when we touch the fruits, the heat of the sun scalds our tired fingers, and we come tumbling down. At such moments, the only witness to our pains is the MIND, which, with continuous pounding shrinks everyday. Yet they tell us that we need the mind to survive, to grow, to overcome the backwardness of our race. It's all a shadow, a vain shadow. What they tell us, and the things that they actually do. The difference can occupy the land between Accra and Rabat!

Obi came to see me yesterday and passionately urged me to write poetry, resume writing poetry that is. He said I must let off steam and return to the ways of the past, when we locked ourselves in that sane innocence, the madness of creativity. Sanity, he argues can only be maintained in this manner. I don't agree, and I don't disagree either. He said something like understanding Ayi Kwei Armah's man in personal terms. And I replied that I saw that man coming into our country many years ago. Now, he sits permanently in every man who tries to live like a man.

The colour green! Anytime I see it blood gushes into my head. And because green is everywhere, my head is always filled. My knees develop a peppery sensation, spreading down my legs. Under my feet, there is a fire burning, roasting me even when the weather is extremely cold. At night, I wake up four times sometimes just to dip my feet into cold water. As for my legs, they feel like those of a hungry mosquito bearing an over-fed giant. When I walk, I feel as if I would crumble in the next ten minutes.

That natural urge to lock horns with a beautiful woman has vanished in a puff of smoke. Even from the subconscious I no longer wish for the standing breasts of a woman as I used to. I no longer see them in my dreams. When I see a beautiful woman flashing her weapons at me, blood fills my large head and I say 'Get thou behind me.' My fingers have tiny needles inside them, piercing me each time I stay still. My eyes flutter involuntarily like a caged weaverbird's.

In the mornings, I don't feel like leaving the bed. Yet, when I remain in bed, I become sick all over. I feel as if the world is going to collapse on my head. Different things crawl inside my body, my head and my arms. The doctor says I must control my thoughts and take things as they come, and prescribes some yellowish tablets. When I take them, everything slows down into a crawl.

I have a bath and feel better. It is a cold bath, which I summoned courage to take because I thought I had fever. The cold bath drives away the fever. This can't be real fever, I tell myself. Everything is hazy around me, as if a jet plane has fouled the atmosphere with a cloudy substance.

The words of the preacher pound into my head:

> I will send it health and cure.
> And I mutter: Time is running out!

Sometimes, I believe that everything has become hazy in the country. I refuse to plan; I refuse to project into a future that may not come. I refuse to see the pain that is tomorrow. Yesterday's bitterness and today's anger do not encourage me to look beyond the present. What shock I would suffer if THEY annulled tomorrow.

At the bus stop, I stare at everyone. They seem to be serious about something. And I ask myself: what are they serious about? Some people move away from me.

A bus arrives. There is a rush, a mad one. Even those who had moved away when I asked my question: 'serious about what?' all rush too. I ask again: 'rush for what'? There is space for one. Fourteen people scramble for it. One person gets it, a sluggish-looking woman. The smile on her face! It shames the gorillas around who had attempted to shove her. Five minutes later another bus arrives, a big empty bus. About twenty of us are left. Another rush. A woman's head-tie comes loose. A young man's shoes come off. They all rush in. I calmly walk in and sit down. I stare back and they adjust themselves on the seats. And I ask myself: am I odd?

We get to the central terminus. The sluggish looking woman is talking away with a very fat man as if the world ends there.

And life continues, its scarcities, its hunger, its loves, and its hatreds. The usurpations are all there, perhaps in abundance.

Uniforms serve as the proclamation of power. Power which was stolen and which would someday be vomited and creep into the crevices of the earth completely naked.

Last week, there was the usual television exhortation, calling on all citizens to be patriotic. The General in charge of Defence was shown to making a speech, saying amongst other things, that men in uniform must learn to respect civil authority in the forthcoming order of things. In the same footage, some activists who had been arrested for forming a political party without government permission were shown being flogged by recruits in the Army. I switched off the set.

Bojor, I know that you are capable of grasping my ramblings. Writing to you eases the heartache I have when I see the monkeys parading themselves as leaders here. When I am alone, my fears overtake me. I feel something running inside my nerves. On my right arm shoulder, there is a flow of excess current, going back and forth, in short sporadic jerks, as if it is the only way that power can come into the arm. It is as if there is too much blood in my system. The psychiatrist says there is a chemical imbalance in my brain, which can be cured through resting and medication.

Rest. How can anyone rest when the heat is enough to burn off clothes? Sometimes I sleep in Sapele, but my mind travels to Ughelli, through Warri, visiting with hungry relations, carrying their sorrows on hunchbacks. In the morning, my mind returns but my body cannot move.

Enough about my sorrows! How are the men of the land treating you? The memories of your last days at home linger on and I know that you are more relevant to the struggle where you are. Your face appears to me every night. Maybe it's because I think of you all the time. Tyrants can only stop deeds. They cannot stop thoughts. I am sure you will remain in the thoughts of compatriots for all eternity.

Yours in the struggle,

Oseme Brughoro.

Bojor never received this letter. The poisonous fangs of the nation's redeemers had arrested his heartbeats on the night that I wrote it. I did not know this, until later, much later….

1

The first time I saw Bojor Aruedon, he was a silhouette, a vague form sitting under a tree, the tree, watching the waves of the quiet lagoon. The lagoon itself looked immense, like a fat goddess waiting for souls to drink into her soul, and he was a priest standing guard at the gate, keeping the people from the hungry mouth of deity, the deity which made people drown in the river of time. He looked a figure suspended in space, dark against the dull-bright background of the firmament. From where I stood, I could see the reflection of the fading sun on the river. An artist trying to capture the scenery on canvas would have to superimpose unknown images on nature in order to enter the spirit of the atmosphere. Sun on sun, sun on moon, and moon on sun, night on day, and the glistening darkness of night on the beauty of the afternoon. A few metres from him, on the floor something glittered, occasionally losing its shine and regaining it as I walked in the direction of the shadow. Its colour changed as well, from gold to grey as I encountered this drop of religion on the soil of freedom. When I got close enough to examining the glittering object, it was the remnant of a crucifix, the only telltale of a moment of passion between two lovers, perhaps, the previous day.

He was chanting some incantations, or so I thought at the time. Later, I came to know that it was the gestation period of his poetic compositions, which came in fitful bouts, at odd times. At such times, he would dramatically stop whatever he was doing and head for the solitude of the pacifying lagoon. Some said Bojor was an eccentric fellow, a man given to the moods of ecstatic happiness and intense depression. One fellow who claimed to know him said he was an alcoholic, a lone drinker who sometimes smoked *ganja* before embarking on any worthwhile venture.

and they spun myths and stories about him,
even though they did not know him;
the lies became truths, as night fell on them.

His happy moods were frequent during the rains. He made conversation so easily on all subjects, including his person and his physiology that one was embarrassed listening to him. All of this came later.

That evening, the sun was beginning to set. It had a bright yellow, golden colour as it reflected in the water. Occasionally I would hear sounds of water hitting the little sand bars created on the banks of the lagoon. Often it reminded me of a dog lapping water from a bowl. Positioned against the sun, Bojor looked like a mystical figure straight from the land of water spirits. His shrill, feminine voice sometimes filtered into my ears, aided by the soft wind that gave the atmosphere an eerie feeling. To the far right, a young couple were neck deep in acts they would sooner or later get tired of.

how long will the stain remain in the cloth
that was set apart for acts of purification?
till they burn the altar and kill the prophets?

If Bojor was aware of their presence, he did not show it. He wore a serious, concentrated look on his face, which I came to know, was his way of keeping his thoughts together.

I sat on the bough of a fallen tree, a few metres away from the dark spirit. I preferred the particular spot where he sat; from there I would enter into myself, seeing myself as I was, as I should be, far from the noise of the powerful men who controlled the land. In fact, if he had not planted himself in the alcove of the shrubs, I would have secured myself there, safe in the arms of nature. I hoped my presence would disturb him. Instead, his intensity increased as time flew by, his voice rendering something like

Alcove of the dream
In the secret recesses
of sacrifice
shall be my testimony

filtered into my ears. My meditation was temporarily arrested by the passion in his voice, arresting also my bubbling spirit which was urging me to commit lines to a sheet of paper. Again his voice came…

and they shall swear
by the handle of the gourd
that the offering
was for the land
locked in battle with
the demons of power...

and drifted away again. For some moments he stayed glued to a particular spot, staring into space. In that interval, I regained myself and went into the deep things of the soul.

Bread does not give life, and life is not made of bread. Without bread, life is a stone; yet its river must flow on to carry the remnants of the struggle. For peace, we must return and face the altar of hope.

That evening, I wrote two poems, which I later showed to Bojor when we became soul brothers in the search for the shell which gave meaning to our lives. He gave a smile and asked me to send a copy to some journal, which I cannot remember now.

The faint sound of a melancholic guitar came into my ears. I guess we both heard the sound at the same time because Bojor stiffened like a rabbit that sensed danger. The guitarist was singing a sad tune in a melancholic but clear voice. The words were not clear but I caught something like 'dem bomb our people for money' and 'Babylon shall fall to rise no more.' It took some time for the guitarist to appear. When he did, he was a frail-looking young man wearing well-packed dreadlocks. His eyes took in the scene, and as he moved towards us, the song took on more urgency. Perhaps it was the intensity of my emotions that made me feel the urgency. The frail singer looked serene. Around his neck was a muffler in bright yellow, red and green colours. When he got in front of me, he paused for a while and greeted:

'Peace, brother.'

'Peace,' I replied, amazed that I could spontaneously give an appropriate reply. He smiled and moved on. On getting to where Bojor sat, he let the guitar loose and shook hands with him. As I found out later, they always had a mystic rendezvous at this spot.

'You can't manage, brother.'

'Can't manage,' Bojor replied.

It became our refrain, this inability to cope with the vanity and oppression in the world. In it we summed our rejection of the dog-eat-dog mentality, which our generation was born into and encouraged to develop. Our guitar friend, who quoted from the book of the Ecclesiastes, provided the spiritual dimension:

To every thing there is a season,

and a time to every purpose under the heaven.
A time to be born, and a time to die;
A time to plant, and a time to pluck up that
which is planted;
A time to kill, and a time to heal;
A time to break down, and a time to build up.
A time to weep, and a time to laugh;
A time to mourn, and a time to dance.
A time to love and a time to hate;
A time of war, and a time of peace.

Somehow we knew that it would all end someday.

In the beginning, we were three, Bojor, Opuda, and I. Later Ovigwe joined us, and we became four. Towards the end of our days on campus, we became five when Obiozor joined us. The four young men and a girl sitting under the almond tree at the lagoon front became a familiar sight to regular to visitors. Ovigwe was a girl among girls.

* * *

Ovigwe met Bojor at a workshop organized by the British Council for upcoming artistes. She was a budding, shy poet with a sense of cryptic humour. Often quiet perhaps due to her stuttering, she had a sharp mind that could catch up very fast on any subject. An actor from Britain was touring the West African coast, exhibiting his talents in demonstrating the character of Shakespeare's Othello. One of his stops was the capital, then a centre for ever-hungry artistes in search of one activity or the other.

They were heady days; those days when we would gravitate from one production to another, miserably and perpetually broke. Between productions we would accumulate debts, mainly around the National Theatre where beer gulped the lion's share of our hard-earned artistes fees. The fees were hopelessly inadequate, yet we clung to the dreams that one day we would transform things, we would be Nigerian-Hollywooders. But hunger was always a sad companion. In fact, I came to suspect that some artistes attended the seminars and workshops mainly to attack the inviting snacks that came at break time.

The faces were usually the same. We usually talked big, with the glow of bright dreams glistening in our eyes. Often the inspirations were more profound when beer coursed through our veins. Then we would see ourselves as superior beings who understood the deep nature of things, of feelings and emotions. We would sit till the wee hours of the morning, lambasting the insensitivity of the government on social issues. The iron-faced Generals in charge of the nation's affairs made a mockery of leadership. Their claims to discipline made the national calamity a tragic-comedy.

> *you cannot dream my dream, even if you control my life.*
> *if they bomb me your father will not save your mother;*
> *and if they kill your father I shall take the horn of the bull*
> *which they cannot control.*

We were custodians of surreal things, unknown to those stuffy fellows who paraded the streets wearing suits and ties. Because we were always laughing, we considered ourselves as people getting the best of life more than those stone-faced leaders whose dedication to duty inspired no hope in their citizens.

* * *

Owen, the name of the actor, did a one-man show of Othello, using masks, change of voice, costumes and make-up to present Shakespeare's great tragic character. It was all fantastic and educative. Looking at him perform, we did not fail to lament the inadequacy of our system, the dearth of theatrical facilities in our country. Certain things, which were described to us in textbooks, became real as Owen lifted the Moor out of Shakespeare's text. Once, a lighting expert had come into the country on the sponsorship of the British Council. He demonstrated the limitless possibilities of lighting effects with the portable equipment which he brought, and we had visions of really transforming the theatre in our country.

Siloko, Bojor, Anighoro, (Ani for short) Opuda, Biodun Shata, Ovigwe, Obiozor, all of us. Optimism was high in spite of the inclement political climate. At the end of such sessions we would emerge with our noses in the air, rich in the new knowledge which the hustling men in suit and tie, looking like over-fed toads did not have. In those days we wore no ties. In fact, anyone who wore a tie was deemed to have joined "them", "them" being soft over-fed bourgeois parasites, whose main interest in life was to acquire capital and oppress the masses. Once a prominent writer met me at the premises of the leading newspaper in the country. I had gone for a job interview, a situation that compelled me to string the rope round my neck.

'Anything the matter?'

It took me some seconds to understand the innuendo in the question.

We were committed to art, and art became a sacred word, a peculiar world in which we lived. Big money was never dreamt of, perhaps because the system itself had pauperised us.

if I raise my sword to harvest paw paw, it will hit
rock stone; so they tell me.

Back to the precincts of the National Theatre, the usual debate would start.

'If we do not like the money-hustlers, and should not associate with them, how then do we get money to transform the theatre from a house of poverty?' Siloko argued.

'Somebody has been enchanted by some money-queen,' a mischievous fellow joked.

'If you want to accumulate capital, don't use the theatre as an excuse. Just go out and join them.' Everyone laughed at Anighoro's rejoinder.

'You see, theatre is not synonymous with poverty. We need money, brothers we need money to transform theatre. But it must be money generated by the theatre, not a donation from some rich fat pig who has looted the economy of the country,' Bojor lectured. 'Ultimately, theatre has to pay its way. No harm at all in making money in the theatre.'

'You have a point there,' I cut in, 'but all over the world there are grants from foundations for the Arts. We need such grants now in our country to give theatre a firm footing.'

'In the civilized world, your argument would be tenable; your idea can only work in a civilized environment. But as long as we have these baboons at the helm of affairs, we cannot afford to nurse such dreams.'

We would go on and on, and sometimes before the end of the night, a particularly drunken fellow would oppose the position that he had canvassed earlier in the day. Biodun Shata was particularly guilty of this. A theatre artist to the core, he was a singer, dancer and actor whose voice took on a life of its own while on stage. The power of his memory in lines-study was so high that years after a production, he would still easily recite some of the lines, particularly while inspired by the richness of Guinness stout.

'Shata, but in the beginning you argued that the rich patrons are rogues who should be avoided. Why should we approach them now and make them finance the revolution?' Ovigwe asked.

'Lady smart, forget what I said earlier on. Mama Tunji, one more Guinness,' he bellowed.

'Sha-ta! You've not paid for what you consumed before.'

'Don't worry. My account will be completely settled before the end of week.' And of course, Mama Tunji obliged him and added another tick to his name on the register.

even the last days of a dying man can light up the
life of the living.

* * *

When Ovigwe heard Bojor speak, she heard the sound of poetry from an oracle of love. We could all see that magic reflected in her large eyes anytime he went into such subjects as polygamy, love, accumulation of wealth, military dictatorships, poverty in Africa and his greatest love, literature.

He had very strong views on military dictatorships. Once he argued — 'I still believe that that buffoon who ruined Uganda through his murderous government should be tried and punished. He cannot destroy innocent lives and take refuge in another country.'

'Our own dictators manage to remain with us,' I chipped in.

'Yes. Ultimately, the people will try them. It may take an age but they will be brought to book before a court and duly punished for treasonably taking over power. For now they call the shots. But one thing is clear: in our statute books coup making is a treasonable offence. The current situation in which a successful coup stamps legitimacy on the act itself will come to an end.'

On poverty in Africa, he opined:

'If African leaders can infuse sincerity and genuine commitment to leadership, a fifty-year plan will wipe out poverty from the continent. Africa has no business being poor with all the resources she is endowed with.'

I remember once the discussions at the lagoon front drifted to poetry and its effect on the soul.

'The romantics indeed enjoyed life in full. Listen to Emily Dickinson: 'if I feel as if my head wants to burst, then I know it is poetry. You know how you feel when you are in love? That is poetry.'

'But such emotions are temporary. You cannot feel as if your head wants to burst everyday of the year. You'll go mad,' somebody countered.

11

'Then you were in love from the first moment,' Bojor replied. 'You see, that which you genuinely love gives you delight anytime you see it.'

'What if her beauty starts to fade, your love can't be the same,' challenged Shata.

'That's where you err. You love the exterior, the externals of the tomb, the faɜade. True love loves the content, the character, the spirit,' Bojor explained.

'You forget brother that character itself changes. It fades. People change. Sometimes the beautiful caring girl you married ends up being a nagging adult, a matronly and all-too proper-woman,' I said. 'What do you do in such a circumstance? Keep loving an absolutely unlovable character?'

I could see in the anger in his eyes, suggesting that my remark was unfair on my uncle, Oneya Obelikpeyah, the civil servant who had eleven children. He always accused me of particularizing arguments when all he was interested in was the principle.

'Brughoro, that is a shame coming from you. Listen that which you really love is permanent. It is always there. Circumstances may affect the way she behaves to you, but it means that the beauty of the truth in her character has to be tapped continuously.'

'It's a two-way thing. She should also learn to tap the thing inside me,' I fired back.

'You are selfish.'

'As far as I am concerned,' came Ade's voice, 'all what you have been talking about is bullshit. Love! It does not bring food to the table. As long as tyrants rule over us, who can practise love? True love can only be practised in a democratic environment. There has to be a thorough transformation of social relations for real harmony to exist.'

'You can't reduce everything to economics. Love is a feeling not a science,' Ovigwe ventured, one of the rare occasions she could contribute to our intense debates.

'True we shouldn't reduce love to economics, but you can smoothen it and cushion its painful aspects with money,' I countered.

Whenever I did this, Bojor was never happy. Apparently everything meant a lot to him. He never believed that I should take a position in an argument in order to oil the discussion. To quote him, 'that is intellectual prostitution'. Once he told me:

'Sometimes it is difficult to place you, you know. You seem to have many sides to your coin.'

'Well that's me! I'm not a reductionist. Life flows in multiple directions. To reduce the energy dynamics of man into rigid principles is denying him his fluid nature,' I countered.

'You are a lost cause!'

when they returned from captivity, they did not know their
God anymore, and they burnt their children as sacrifice to other
gods.

At such times Ovigwe would simply look into his eyes, saying nothing, knowing that we were deeply committed to each other. She believed as she once told me that we must be frank to each other, brutally so, to sustain the essence of our relationship. I admired him for his zest for life, and his ability to go into the spirit of things, of discussions. There was no detachment during these times. When Ovigwe's mother died, he felt more than Ovigwe herself, who found strength in the weakness of this intellectual giant. Perhaps this was what made their love what it was. Ovigwe gave up all claims to class superiority by sticking to an eccentric artist. She changed her dress style, becoming boyish in the process. She stopped going to church, claiming that the love which the preacher gave was too abstract. The only day she spoke about her withdrawal from church, she was emotional, yet so fluent. I remember that day clearly. We had gone for the funeral of an artiste who died while carving an image of a mighty tree. His technique was an innovation. With the aid of saw blades, cutlasses, hammers, nails and all tools a carpenter could not boast of, he would create a unique statue that stood on its natural feet.

One day, after spending some fourteen odd hours on the tree, he decided to come down. Ordinarily, this took him less than five minutes. But that day was a black day; he missed a branch and landed on the ground with a heavy thud. It was late in the night, and because he was working alone, help did not come. He was unconscious, bleeding through the nose. When help came in the morning, he was mid-way between life and death. On the way to the hospital, they ran into a road block mounted by footmen of the reigning day, still searching for some renegade soldiers who had tried to overthrown their Commander -in- Chief. It took two hours for the road to clear. Time in which Banji Origbo, artist *par excellence*, slipped into bliss. Discipline was the watchword. If the car (well it was not an ambulance) had tried to drive on the other lane that carried traffic from the opposite direction, the driver and passengers (including the dying artist) would have been thoroughly flogged, after being asked to frog jump.

In fact, while in the 'go slow,' Banji's uncle had gone to one of the soldiers to plead that they be allowed to pass through because they were carrying an injured man. The stern look which the soldier gave him, almost made him shit in his pants.

* * *

'Him be my oga.'

'No sir, no officer. It's Banji, Banji Origbo the artist, the man who won the National Merit Award last year. He is in a car, at the back of this... please allow us ...' Banji's uncle could not finish.

'Sergeant!' a voice bellowed.

'Yessir!'

'What's that bloody civilian arguing with you about sir?'

'Him want preferential treatment?'

'Preferential treatment? Vanish from here. You scallywag! But for your age I would have taught you a good lesson. Disappear now!'

The old man, already shivering, jerked in reaction to the last barked order. He tripped over a stone on the ground, fell, tried to rise again, much to the amusement of the on-lookers. At last, he managed to stand, ran a few metres, and relapsed into a casual walk. He shook his head from side to side.

'These soldiers will kill all of us.'

In a music shop on the other side of the road, a voice was singing, bellowing forth its message with an angry resonance, 'Na double wahala for dedi body.'

who can I hold responsible for the slaughter of the victims of war;
the commander barked at the sergeant to let loose the canons of death when the children asked for bread. These were our saviours from the tyranny of democracy.

* * *

Artistes all over the country organized funeral ceremonies. In their gatherings, they condemned the action of the soldiers at the checkpoint. They complained about the ill-treatment meted out to the artist, and that it was unbecoming for an artist of Banji's stature to die in a traffic jam caused by security men searching for escaping coup plotters. As a form of defiance, the artists held a vigil, reading poems and short stories from radical literature. The Association of Authors made a presentation of selected readings and gave cash donations to his children. A leading musical artiste brought the celebration to an end by giving a heart-rending version of "We own the world.' All of us rose in one accord and held hands to symbolise the bond of unity that held all artistes. It went on and on until our poet Bojor gave the final word. I remember that night clearly. The concluding line read thus:

> *if I take my exit while my fire is burning*
> *it is because the smoke of life will light up*
> *the rest of the world so let it be.*

The report was all over the newspapers. Most editors were cautious about the scope of publicity which they gave the dead man's transition. At that time, it was a criminal offence to publish anything, true or false, which could embarrass the government. Only one newspaper had the courage to condemn the whole episode, blaming the soldiers for being insensitive to human feelings. Three days later, a mysterious explosion rocked the newspaper house. Although no one died, not a single printing machine survived the onslaught.

* * *

The Reverend Pastor who officiated at Banji's funeral ceremony was an eloquent, well-fed, robust looking middle-aged man. His cheerful face gave the impression of a man who was always in a party mood. He was one of the products of the new generation churches that had come to dominate the country in the midst of a deep economic recession. They preached miracles, claiming that they had the powers to liberate men from the clutches of the devil. During the sermon, Ovigwe barely stopped herself from shouting to the priest that he should bother himself about freeing people from the clutches of poverty and the devils that run our national affairs than some spirit, mystical, or mythological, who took all the blame for the evils that man did. What irked Ovigwe most was the theme of love, which the priest preached while burying a man of peace whose death was caused by official tyranny and hatred.

'Let us turn our cheek,' he had exhorted. 'Let us practise love and pray for them. Let us support them to build a well-disciplined nation where no man is oppressed ...'

It was too much for Ovigwe. She tapped Bojor on the arm.

'Let's get out of here.'

'Why?' Bojor asked, engrossed in his own thoughts. But when he looked at Ovigwe's eyes, he knew that he must leave. They went outside the church, and strolled to the gravesite. Later, much later, when they brought the corpse for burial, above everything else, the sight of nine little kids left behind by the thirty-nine year old artist to mourn him,

15

along with their six mothers, touched Ovigwe. Cute little things, they took their turns paying their last respects to their father. Very few people that day could restrain their tears.

i bequeath you nothing but the power of the pen;
bring down the mighty men of violence; for this will
be the greatest legacy you will leave behind
as a testament to freshness of the umbilical.

Back at Mama Tunji's, we drank to quench our thirst and submerge our sorrows.

'This doctrine of turning your cheek while men and women like us perpetrate evil in the name of leadership does not agree with my sensibilities. I quit church until the revolution.'

'An additional soul lost,' quipped Bojor.

'Not to the devil, luckily. Ovigwe's firm belief in God remains. She only quarrels with fools,' I said.

'Hardly any difference,' Bojor replied dryly. 'If you blame the fools, you must blame the workman for choosing such fools.'

'I understand God's patience with all men; else we would all be dead by now. What offends my soul is the farcical show being put up by men masquerading as agents of God. Christ himself acknowledges the need for a revolution. Our Preachers should preach the coming of a Moses. This Moses must be one of us,' Ovigwe argued. All through the period I had known her, she had never expressed any opinion with so much feeling. It increased her stammer.

* * *

At the British Council, Bojor had just presented a poem in the post-workshop socialization. As usual, the critics were there to praise or condemn the poem, depending on their level of ignorance or knowledge. It was a love poem, tinged with the absolutely realistic images of social concern. Bojor replied the critics, basing his reaction on the existence of feelings even in time of political and economic oppression. At the end of the session, Ovigwe confronted Bojor with some questions about his writing style. The discussion that followed lasted three hours. More than anything else, Bojor loved her spirit, her fighting spirit and her intellectual honesty. It was the beginning of a new relationship that went on for years, till a physical separation that led Bojor on a spiritual pilgrimage across the Atlantic.

'I'm Bojor,' the frail man introduced himself.

'Brughoro, is my name,' I said. 'Bru for short.'

'How are you, Bru?'

'Fine. And you?'

'Surviving.'

'The guitarist. We haven't met before, have we?'

'No brother no. Me no know how dem and me go make things work,' the guitarist replied. 'Wada is my name.'

It was the beginning of a new friendship for the three of us. Throughout the years on Campus, the lagoon front provided a rallying point for us, particularly when we could not afford the bus fare to go to the National Theatre where we were creditworthy. Sometimes at night after reading for hours, we would go to the lagoon front, Ovigwe joining us as usual. Often, Wada would entertain us with his soulful compositions. We would all be silent, listening to our inner souls, at peace with our spirits.

In a way, it was an escape from the harsh realities of the world. Out there, we saw ourselves, as we were, naked, vulnerable, but strong in spirit. After Ovigwe joined us, we no longer lacked money. And so we no longer lacked food. She was a great provider though a bad cook, which she attributed to her bourgeois upbringing. Once she prepared something, which she called fried rice and brought it to our 'restoration shrine,' (for that was the name we gave the place where we rejuvenated our spirits). Because there was usually frankness in our relationships, we pushed the hard rice aside and fell on the chicken with hungry anger. After that, she never attempted to cook for us any more.

Rarely did Bojor and Ovigwe sit apart whenever we went to the shrine. We were always together, yet individually apart, until much later with palm wine swimming in us as lost conversation came back. Later, much later, marijuana came into the restorative meeting. As for me, I dragged on it once and knew that my mind could not accommodate its high potency. I coughed and coughed, managing to laugh in the process, at myself, at the others. And it was all fun. But I never touched it after that. The others all left me alone, respecting my right to self-motivated inspiration at the shrine of restoration. As for Ovigwe, she took a drag once and slept for three days. We were so alarmed that we called a medical student friend of ours who assured us that she would sleep it off. On the third day, she woke up, ate a huge meal and promptly returned to the business of taking lectures and loving her friend.

Wada was the master of marijuana. Bojor occasionally inhaled its fumes, waxing eloquent after the experience. After reading Armah's novel, Bojor decided to explore the truth in wee-wee, as the writer described it and how it made thoughts clear. Bojor could tolerate it, though we could see that he did it mainly to keep Wada going as a member of the group. Throughout it all, Obiozor never touched the stuff. He believed as a result of strict parental upbringing that if he as much as inhaled the stuff, he would run mad. Nothing could make him change his mind.

> *some chains come from the womb, mother-born;*
> *some come from the mind, attitude-born;*
> *some are born by the minions who hold power.*

Years later, when Wada died suddenly in his sleep, everyone concluded that he had died as a result of *ganja* abuse.

2

Shortly after Bojor and I became friends, we both travelled to his village to see his aged father and young mother. As was usual with us in those days, we tried to make our visit as dramatic and eventful as possible. The decision to travel was made on a Friday evening after we returned from a poetry reading session at the Poetry Club Village somewhere in the outskirts of the city.

At the park, we boarded a Benin-bound bus along with fourteen other passengers. It was going to be a night journey because the time was already 4.30pm. The union workers at the park were extra active that evening, perhaps because it was Friday. In the last three years, the downward turn in the economy separated families, causing one parent to work in one town while the wife and children lived in another. It created a new concept of family, re-defining the notion of family head and unity. Some husbands started new families in the process. Often the wife at home did not know about the other family. To keep the 'main wife' from knowing about her mate, the husband had to travel home fairly regularly. So Fridays were a bonus to the agberos who took advantage of the situation to hike fares. The world of agberos was a different one, what with their rules and regulations that ran counter to the laws of the land. Officially, they were no longer allowed to operate as a union after a battle of attrition between rival groups in the union. The government had to step in only after the leader of a faction was murdered in cold blood as he alighted from his car at home after the day's business. Newspaper reports claim that the murder was so brutal that it was actually planned to take place in front of his children. Three little kids had run out to welcome 'daddy' only to witness two men emerge from a car that had been parked in front of their home, pump bullets into their father. Calmly, the two men boarded their car and drove off. Residents ran into their houses, shutting their doors with great trepidation, and thanking God that it did not happen to them. One of the children was the first to come out after the assassins left. A boy of not more than ten years old, he took his father's head on his thighs and started crying. It was only then that adults came out to drag the boy from the dead man. He kept asking: 'where is the toy you said you would buy for me? Daddy! Daddy!'

Years later it was reported that the boy never recovered from the shock of seeing his father murdered because he would run along the road and ask an imaginary daddy for his toy.

they say madness runs in the family of the weak heads;
whose head can remain strong when trauma eats up the flesh of the mind?

The police stepped in and told the press that investigations were on. Two days on, the newspapers reported that the leader of the rival gang had been kidnapped. A search for him started. Exactly twenty-four hours after he was kidnapped, his wife received a phone call from him asking her to come alone to a particular address to pick him up. Somehow, she beat the police net and arrived at an uncompleted building in the remote area of the city. She entered the empty sitting room and was surprised by the bloodstains all over the house. She did not need to go far. Inside one of the empty bedrooms lay the body, or what was left of it, the head severed from the body. She fainted.

That evening, the union was banned. Its officials were arrested. In no time, they were released and it was business as usual. Now, they have returned in another guise to operate as kings of the park.

We set out for Orereame. Bojor and I sat in the middle seat with two voluptuous ladies who let anyone that cared to listen know that they were undergraduates. As the journey progressed, we became friends, finding a common interest in the topical issue of the day, whether the military was indeed keen on handing over power to civilians. Bojor was sceptical, saying that it was not in the tradition of military leaders to willingly abdicate from power.

'It runs counter to their training. Besides, it is clear that they do not have any respect for the politicians.'

'You forget that in Ghana, the military Head of state handed over power to a democratically elected government and returned to the barracks,' one of the girls said.

Some passengers made their contributions and we were divided into two groups. While some were convinced that the military was sincere, others prophesied a sudden about-face in the leaders' plan towards disengagement.

*all we can do is talk while their long fingers dig into
mother's pot of soup, eating the meat, flinging us bones.*

We arrived in Orereame at about 9.15 pm, much to the relief of Bojor who had a morbid fear of accidents. He always believed that he would die in an accident. As a result, he used to get boozed up before travelling. That way, he was able to keep himself from fainting from fear.

*sometimes the dark spots of our mind light up
the world of the unknown, and we argue with fate.*

As we alighted from the bus, it was obvious that the two girls expected us to invite them to our place. Bojor, admirer of only slim girls quickly moved on as if he had suddenly realised that he was late for his appointment. When I teased about how he had quickly abandoned the ladies, he said something about being consistent in taste. Slim girls gave him a kind of weakness that he could not understand.

We found our way to his brother's place somewhere in Akporona area. It was late and his brother's wife did not fail to remind us it was not safe to move at night. This she did in a rude manner, looking battle ready. We ignored her, declined an offer of a meal and locked ourselves in the guest room. His brother had travelled to the next village. Very early in the morning we set out for Tosafe, the last major town on the coast of the Delta. From there we boarded a boat for Bojor's village, the place from which he said he derived his poetic genius.

was this white soup prepared inside a black pot?

Orereame was a small island in the creeks leading to the Atlantic. It was a different world to me, having been away from the Delta for a long time. The speedboat we boarded took about fifteen passengers though it was meant for was ten. When somebody complained about the possibility of the boat capsizing, the boatman replied:

'So what, if boat capsize, we go swim go for shore or you dey fear to enter inside water?'

Suddenly everyone in the boat started speaking at the same time.

21

'Foolish man! If you no value your life, then make you jump into the river,' cried the woman.

'God punish you; make you take your mouth talk nonsense again and see wetin I go do you.'

'You wan beat me inside my boat? Make una come see me see trouble.'

I was enraged and frightened at the same time. There he was seated calmly in the back of the boat speeding in crocodile-infested water and talking glibly about a boat capsizing. I controlled my anger when I saw that he wore a mischievous smile on his face. He stopped replying the rain of insults that followed. Instead, he smiled. Then I caught on. It was a joke to him. I was particularly frightened because I could not swim. Bojor did nothing to reassure me until he calmly declared that if there were an accident he would carry me on his back and swim to the shore. The mere thought of it gave me the shivers I'd rather not be in a capsized boat and get saved by my gallant friend. I did not realize that I spoke aloud, because Bojor replied:

'It happens daily here and the people are used to it. They understand what it is to rescue drowning people.'

'Do you mean that there will be a rescue team if this boat suddenly develops a problem?'

'Sure. Our people have their own ways. It may not be as organized as you want it. But here it is compulsory for good swimmers to help drowning people as a matter of course. So you can see that the river is better than road travelling. Here I can save you. Road accident? Gbam and its all over. If one does not sustain any injuries, he'll be too shocked to give help,' he concluded.

'Don't be too certain about swimming to safety. The best swimmers usually die while swimming,' I told him.

The whole thing appeared morbid to me. All the talk about drowning brought frightful images to me, particularly an experience I had as a boy at the riverside.

whenever I see the carvings on my father's back,
i remember the shape of our history.

It was just after the civil war. Almost everything was in short supply, including kerosene and gas. Families resorted to cooking with firewood. The town where I lived with my uncle was a remote part of town, which had come to assume features of a modern city. Life was simple and uncomplicated. One could walk with his head looking down, not fearing about a car knocking one down. Yet there were some claims to

22

class because some professional wood-fetchers would go into the forest to bring wood. Some families depended on these men who paddled their boat across the river, cut firewood from the mangrove forest and brought them back for sale to the retail sellers, usually women.

I always accompanied my uncle's wife to the local port where the men deposited the wood right into the waiting arms of the women. I became familiar with the type of wood that would easily burn. The one called ikpaya was usually a last resort. It burnt too fast because it was brittle. It was also difficult to split. I knew this because it was my duty to split firewood, using an axe. As man of the house, I was expected to cut the wood into bits so that they could fit into the hub, the ogaga.

On this day, auntie was haggling with the wood seller. I slipped away and sat peacefully on a jetty a few metres away watching soldiers take their bath in the river. They were rather noisy and boisterous, doing everything with a crude confidence that scared us. These men were a part of the second set of soldiers to arrive in the town, ostensibly to secure it against enemy takeover. But they were not friends at all because women, married and unmarried were not safe as long as they stayed in the town. Some women were forcefully taken away from their husbands, much to the disappointment of the "liberated" people. Why should we supporters of the Federal side suffer such degradation?

To return to the present, the soldiers barked at each other, hitting out at and generally fooling around while swimming. These were strange men, men who had actually fought a war and killed thousands of men from the rebel enclave.

> *they put on green uniforms, colour of fertility*
> *to kill our lives, and the lives of our enemies.*
> *they say they have come to redeem us from the*
> *fangs of rebels; but they have turned our wives into theirs.*

I admired the way that the soldiers swam and wished that I could be so brave as to swim the way they did. Suddenly one of the soldiers yelled. I cannot remember what exactly he said. Whatever he said brought everyone to a standstill. A few minutes later, two soldiers brought the body of a boy my age from the river and dumped him casually on the slope that led to the jetty. After performing this simple task they went back swimming. I fled the scene.

The women, of course, took over, taking turns to look at the body and weeping in the process. As they went to see the prostrate form, I suppose they did so with mixed feelings.

'Let it not be my son, or the son of somebody that I know,' one of them wailed.

'Oh poor child! What happened to him?'

A returnee said:

'Thank God it's not my son.'

I wondered in my mind whether the boy's mother would have any reason to thank God.

the pastor asked all the survivors to come for thanksgiving; the man who lost his pregnant wife slapped the messenger.

Auntie found me later and squeezed my ear lobes as if I was the person who sent the boy to the river and murdered him. 'You see that corpse, that is what happens to boys who disobey their parents and sneak to secret places. If you ever sneak to the river, that is what will happen to you.'

'But auntie, I ...'

'Shut up your elephant mouth,' she snapped. 'Have you not done worse things?'

* * *

A few hours later, a man rode in on a huge scooter. He was a giant of a man with a big bushy beard that looked very much like the rebel leader's. Dressed in coat and tie, he looked the typical civil servant called away from his duty post to witness a sad scene. He bounced as he walked, giving away his anxiety as he stared in only one direction. When he got to where the body was, his bouncing steps ceased. In his bold, bouncing place was a sad, withered man whose only son had drowned while playing. He broke down in tears, and knelt down before his child's corpse, crying 'Israel, what have you done to me? What have you done? Why? Why?' He was then led away by some men who had witnessed the scene from a distance. The sight unnerved me, and the picture of a boy on the floor, dead, with one arm and leg slightly raised, never left my mind.

Whenever I had the temptation to go the river to swim, I would remember the man crying 'Israel, oh Israel, what have you done to me?' I would then shrink. I did not want to do anything that would cause death and grieve my folks. From then on, I had a kind of river-phobia.

Later, word went round that the boy's parents were separated and that he had just come from his mother's place to spend the long holiday in his father's house, under the care of his stepmother. When somebody said that he was the only male child in a family of nine children, the wood market women concluded that the boy's stepmother must have bewitched the boy into going to drown in the river so that her children would be the ones to inherit her husband's estate.

if they pick up the remnants of my ancestors from
the gangway in Badagry, they will exhibit it in
the beautiful museums of Europe.

'In a few minutes we shall be there,' the voice of Bojor brought me back to the present. 'You'll see my father, a huge man in stature.'

'So where did get your small frame from,' I asked him. Bojor was a diminutive fellow with a forceful personality. Whenever he walked, he took short steps, throwing one leg out first as if he wanted the leg to catch up with world first. His very dark skin was always shiny. Apart from his small stature, his eyes singled him out in any crowd. He had the bright eyes of a wild cat.

'Perhaps I got it from my mother. Just wait till we get there and you will be able to make your assessment.'

Soon we arrived at a roughly constructed jetty. The boatman manoeuvred his boat to a corner, stepped into the water and tied it to one of the pilings of the jetty. From this point, I could not see much of the village, the jetty being on a slope. But as soon as we alighted and I stepped on the jetty, I was compelled to admire the natural beauty of my friend's birthplace.

The entire village looked very familiar, like a place I had been to before. The sand on the ground was white in colour. People went about quietly, and there were a lot of greetings. There were thatch houses standing beside modern ones. Everybody seemed to know Bojor just as he knew everyone.

'Son of the chief, when did you come?'

'I have just arrived.'

'How is school?'

'Fine, Papa.'

Bojor addressed all the men as papa and the women as 'mama.' When I asked him, he explained that it was the community's way of ensuring harmony and respect. A child, who calls one father, will always receive protection from the man. I was enlightened, and enjoyed the logic. What would it look like if I got back to the city and addressed every man as 'Papa' and all women as 'Mama'? Won't they think that I am crazy? I said as much to Bojor.

'Here, the communal ethos is intact. It is not a perfect situation, I know. But our people try to keep to some form of traditional order. Every year, all our sons and daughters come from far and wide. At such times, we reinforce communal harmony.'

'How long do they think this will last?' I asked him as we negotiated a bend.

'I suppose it will last as long as we are all able to keep television and oil explorers from our land.'

I kept quiet for a while as we walked on. The closer we got to his father's house, the stronger the feeling that I had been here before. There were mud houses built in clusters, and a low fence protected each cluster.

'Each cluster houses a family. A family is made of all blood relations, from cousins to grand children.'

'What about a young man who wants to build his own house and live independently?' I asked.

'There is no need for that.' Bojor explained, 'what some men have done is rebuild the family house. These are the houses built with cement.'

At that very moment we encountered a sprawling edifice, constructed along the principles of modern architecture.

'This house, for example, belongs to a retired army officer. He rebuilt this family house a few years ago. Any child of the family who returns home must have somewhere to sleep.'

'I suppose that is how the world ought to be,' I said weakly. 'This dog eat dog thing which we see everyday in Lagos is simply killing.'

'That is why we must return to our traditional values,' Bojor explained, 'though how we can achieve this is not an easy thing.'

'It will definitely not be easy, but we ought to try.'

We turned off from the main road, which ran through the village.

'My father's compound is at the end of this road,' Bojor explained. 'You can see it from here.'

At the end of the road, I saw a compound that looked new. It had a small gate. We entered the compound. In the middle of the compound sat a two-story building, which Bojor said was his father's. Little children were playing in front of it, running about naked with reckless abandon. When they saw Bojor, the sound of 'Brother! Brother! Brother!' filled the air. From the far left of the compound, several women appeared whom I suspected to be Bojor's father's wives. Some were about Bojor's age while others looked old. Greetings took place, a very long ritual. While Bojor went on his knees before some, others knelt down to greet him.

'Migwo,' one would greet.
'Vre do,' the other would reply.
'Oma garen?'
'Doh!'

It went on and on. Somebody took our luggage and we entered the main house. The sitting room was tastefully furnished with upholstered chairs and rugs, a big contrast with the environment. Although the village had no supply of electricity, there was a television set in the sitting room. We were led to a room, which I supposed was where we would both spend our days here.

'Where is Papa?'

'He went to Okopiri to attend a meeting.'

'What time did he leave here?'

'He left here this morning. We expect him back before nightfall.'

After some moments, we were left alone, just the two of us. Bojor had distributed some loaves of bread and packets of biscuits to different children, carefully giving out the gifts according to the 'tree' they belonged. As he explained later, all the children grow up as brothers and sisters. But in giving out gifts, one had to make sure that he did not leave out children born by any of the women. This could be misinterpreted.

It was a bright day and Bojor suggested that we pay a visit to his mother. I was curious to see his mother. We came back to the sitting room, and found our way out. We then moved to the left-hand corner of the compound where I saw a cluster of huts built in the traditional fashion. It was polished with some special kind of mud. The walls were particularly high.

'Papa left this thatch house intact even after he built the modern one. All his wives, including my mother live here.'

'Why don't they all move to the new house?' I asked him.

'The older ones refused to move, preferring the cool comfort of the thatch house. The junior wives took a cue, and decided to remain here.'

' A form of female solidarity!'

'The women must have their reasons for asking to be allowed to stay in the old building,' I said.

'Not really. Some of the young girls have rooms in both places. Sometimes they sneak out to stay in the 'big house' for a day or two and return to their own. That way they keep abreast of all family gossip, which usually take place in the traditional house.'

We arrived. The front of the house was well kept. It had a courtyard, big enough to serve as a basketball pitch. The sitting room itself contained artefacts and some memorabilia. There was a door

27

immediately at the back of the sitting room that led to the inside of the compound. The middle door had an opening. To the left and right hand sides, there were rooms, which I supposed belonged to the wives. By this time the children had crawled around us. The women were outside their rooms, exchanging banter with Bojor. Some of the jokes were rather bawdy.

'Umuko,' Bojor called out. 'You look so young and beautiful. Make sure you don't finish off Papa with your succulence.'

'That one! No woman can finish him off. In fact he can finish off two of any type any day.'

The women all roared in laughter. Somehow, the spirit of happiness around us infected me. If life was this simple, perhaps we should all return to it, I thought. Gradually Bojor meandered us to a room and we both entered and sat down. The room was barely furnished. It had a bed, two wooden chairs and some mats. A few minutes later, one of the young women we had seen outside came in carrying some bottles of drinks.

'Is this your sister?' I asked him. Bojor burst into laughter.

'Sister? She is my mother.' I couldn't believe it. The resemblance between them was striking. Bojor had obviously inherited the shape of her head, her complexion, and her stature. She was so dark that she reminded me of the parable of searching for a black sheep at night.

'Migwo ma,' Bojor said, kneeling fully on the ground.

'Vre do.' I did the same and this caused some laughter, perhaps because, I did not use the right accent. The hostess provided food. The main ingredients were fish and periwinkle. It was delicious.

Bojor and his mother spoke in their native tongue, while I enjoyed the drinks placed before us. There were also drinks from the other women, brought in by their children. Kola nuts also arrived. I did not touch them, having learnt from experience that it was not good for me. Once, at a traditional wedding ceremony, I chewed away only to find myself being unable to sleep till dawn. I tossed about in bed till the early hours of the morning, and then had a fitful sleep. It lasted only ten minutes, or so I thought. I had slept for one hour. From that day on, kola-nut was not for me.

Bojor's mother, Omoteoyibo, sat on her bed, looking shy in front of her grown up son. All her little children sat around on her bed, staring at their big brother. She was the reserved type. As Bojor later told me, she came into marriage at fifteen and had him at sixteen. In fact, there was a special place for her in the house. She was the sixth wife and the one who gave birth to the first surviving son. In a way therefore, Bojor was heir apparent. Later, I teased him.

'Someday you shall inherit all of this.' He caught the message right away, because I had laid emphasis on the women.

'Well, not a bad idea, vulgar reformist,' he replied, 'though I know that before that time comes, events will actually determine who actually inherits what.' Looking back now, that was indeed a prophetic statement.

'Mama, I'll stay for two days. As soon as Papa returns, I'll discuss some issues with him and go back to school.'

'School! School! All your life has been about school, school. When will you settle down, work and enjoy yourself?'

'Mama I enjoy reading. That is my work.'

'Does it fetch you money?'

Bojor had no answer. How could he explain that he wanted to read up to doctorate level before picking up a lecturing job? How could he explain that he was a writer who aspired to create characters that would be known worldwide?

The conversation drifted to other subjects ranging from local politics to the activities of oil companies in other villages.

'Otokutu has electric supply now. There is no night or day there right now. Both have been fused into one by the oil company working there.'

'Really? What about the people? Do they enjoy it?'

'Of course they do. They now call us bush people who have not seen the light,' she said, 'why your father and some elders oppose their coming here to do the same beats my imagination.'

'Has oil been found here too?'

'I don't know for sure. What we do know is that some white people came to see Papa with papers and after they left, he called a meeting. At the end of one the meetings, the chiefs started talking about agreement, agreement. Everything now centres on agreement.' Bojor's mother concluded.'

'The men must have their reason for asking for an agreement.'

'O yes! The people of Otokutu now come for fish. They claim that they can no longer fish in their village. Most of the fish they see are already dead.'

Bojor and I exchanged looks, significantly, because back in the city, we had been involved in an environmental protection agency. For most people, environmental degradation was an abstract term. Oil pollution was exaggerated. Face to face with it in his village, Bojor swore to get into the struggle of freeing his people from the yoke of the oppressors.

'Mama, Papa is correct. The village must ensure that there is an agreement before exploration takes place.'

a piece of paper with a seal may give melodious
tunes to the ears of the oppressed; the oppressor
calls it a farting document of convenience.

We hit the village, though there was not much to see or do. We stopped at a palm wine bar where we helped ourselves to fresh palm wine, bled from the breast of rich, luscious trees. Palm wine here was cheap, compared with what we used to buy it in the city. It was also undiluted. Some of the hard drinkers would saunter and bellow.

'You get overnight?'

'Overnight e dey.'

They could then sit and enjoy themselves with fermented palm wine. Because it was fermented, its intoxicating effects were quicker than fresh palm wine. In the bar, the dominant subject was the coming of the oilmen to the village. Down to the last man, everyone wanted an agreement. After some gourds of palm wine, we went exploring the village.

* * *

In one hour, we had circumnavigated the village. This we did in one of Bojor's father's boats, which we picked up at the jetty, referred to as 'War-f' by the people. It was a beautiful sight to see from the river. There were other villages around, looking like large birds perched on water from a distance. We also encountered speedboats racing to oilrigs, carrying white men and black girls. Somehow, they all seemed to be enjoying themselves, laughing and punching each other while the boat raced on. From the distance we could see huge cylinders from which glowed red flames producing harsh jetty heat. This was the flared natural gas that took place largely in the delta areas. In some villages, huge sums of money were paid to village heads to settle the matter.

Even the leaders wore the uniforms of the enemy,
Calling themselves leaders of the people.

It was evening when we finally returned to the jetty. We walked slowly, discussing all subjects under the sun. The burning issue was the effect of oil exploration. Before now, the level of awareness was indeed low. The villagers freely welcomed oil explorers because their arrival usually brought modern amenities. Sometime, they built roads or health centres manned by a pharmacist. The villagers were quite satisfied with these. However, events in the last few months raised the consciousness of all oil producing communities. Far away in Gedam, the government hanged an activist whose community prevented the explorers from destroying their ancestral homes. Before the hanging, the media had been replete with quotable quotes from his speeches. He gave facts and figures to back up his claim that the oil companies spent less than what they made from communities to help development. He described the schools and health centres built as a mere token. It was an eye opener for the communities. People started asking questions, much to the embarrassment of the government. Things took a dramatic twist when soldiers executed the man in full public glare. He was killed like a common armed robber.

* * *

I remember the incident clearly because I had attended some seminars in which the radical lawyer presented papers, detailing the level of pollution in the delta region of the country. He had maps, photographs, and video recordings to back up his statements. He had still and moving photographs of the largest villages in the history of the country. He was often a guest of the security agents. Usually, the security agents seized most of the documents. Somehow he managed to get more. In fact, the more documents they seized, the more aggressive the lawyer became in getting fresh documents. At a point, the security man gave up.

After he was executed, the government ran into a storm of attacks and criticism. Apparently the government was not aware of how popular he was until after the execution. There was a diplomatic row and ambassadors were recalled. Within the country, editorials condemned the act, enjoying the great embarrassment, which the government was writhing under. The press enjoyed temporary freedom. Because the government could not stand further attacks, it soft-pedalled on detaining editors or banning media organizations.

Overnight, he became a martyr and what the state wanted to avoid by silencing him, became public property. More villages and oil producing communities became emboldened and went to court.

The carcass of a giant tree is booty, even for the weak.

Just before we branched off the road leading to Bojor's father's compound, we saw a small gathering of men and women. They were

31

singing and dancing, producing music by hitting bottles with sharp objects. When Bojor suggested that we should join them, I wondered whether we would be welcomed without an invitation.

'Friend, relax, you are not in the city.' It is a naming ceremony. No one expects to be invited to witness the naming ceremony of his son or brother or sister. It was all so logical to me.

Shortly after we joined the group, the dancing stopped. An elderly man sat in front of the house, supported by other elders. The women were all in one corner. Prominent in front was the mother of the newly-born child. A matronly-looking woman was carrying a baby wrapped in warm clothes. She stood up and gingerly presented the baby to the elder. The Master of Ceremonies called for silence and the elder's voice rang in prayer.

'A child that is born must have a name. A child without a name is a child without a father. A child without a father is a bastard. Do we produce bastards in our homes?'

'No!' everyone replied.

'This child shall be named today. But before I name him, I must say a few things.

God brought this child, and God will provide for him. His left foot will not travel before his right. When he walks into the night, may it become day.'

'Ise!' chorused the audience.

'We have given birth to a baby boy, a human being. But when he steps out into the world, and men become lions, may he have the spirit to become a lion.'

'Ise!'

'May he never travel when the river or the road waits famished.'

'Ise!'

'He is not a sacrificial lamb. When the rioters of this world look for human sacrifice, may he be absent.'

'Ise!'

'He will be the father of many children!'

'Ise!'

'…of grand-children …'

'Ise!'

'…Of great-grandchildren…'

'Ise!

'…of sakpugodin…'

'Ise!'

'He will be the husband of many wives!'

'Ise!'

'He will read books and surpass the white man himself.'

'Ise!'

'A child derives his name from circumstances. We pray that bad circumstances should not surround the birth of our children.'

'Ise!'

'If bad circumstances arise, may we have the courage to face them!'

'Ise!'

'A name is a prayer, a statement, a wish, an identity. May the wish behind his name be fulfilled in our love.'

'Ise!'

'The baby's name is 'Agreement.'

There was a slight drop in the number of 'Ise' that followed the name. The elder seemed to have perceived the drop in spirit. He continued, raising his booming voice to drown the din that followed the announcement of the name.

'May we have a good agreement with those who want to drill our land!'

'Ise!' chorused everyone.

'His other names are Emuejevoke, Ijelekpo and Obominuru.'

There was applause and drinking, in obvious appreciation of the elder's spontaneous reaction to a national situation. That was followed with fresh fish, which we could hardly afford in the city. I ate more fish in two days that I had ever eaten since I was born. By this time, it was dark. Specks of light were everywhere, provided by bush lanterns placed there by the different compounds. It was time to leave for home.

* * *

When we arrived back at Bojor's father's compound, it was really dark. I had to stay close to Bojor to be able to find my way. Inside the compound, bright light flooded the veranda.

'Where did light suddenly come from?' I asked Bojor.

'Up,' he answered casually. 'It's the generator that is switched on only when we have important visitors or during festivals.'

'Who is the important visitor?'

'You want me to flatter you?'

We entered the sitting room and I came face to face with the father of my friend, the chief of the village. He was every inch a royal person, huge, dark, and full of life, the very opposite of my friend. When he shook my hands, I grimaced because he squeezed me too hard.

'Welcome, my sons.' His warmth was infectious. Bojor knelt down to greet him, an action which I immediately copied. He asked us to stand up and take our seats. We looked round to greet the other men in the room. From nowhere a bottle of schnapps appeared, supported by kola nuts, some money, and some bottles of beer. One of the men rose, cleared his throat and began to speak:

'Urhobo, wa do!'

'Eeh'

'Wa do'

'Eeh'

'Olorogun, udova wen!'

'Eto iwen!'

'Eto iwen!'

'You cannot remove me without closing your eyes.'

'Baba. Your praise name?'

'Adjerese!'

'Adjerese!'

'O ye ese!'

'Omo e baba. Udova wen!'

'Oro kpi school!'

'Oro kpi school!'

'O yo ne be!'

'Oyen. E be a rue mu oyen e ruemu. We have our son visiting from school. He is not alone. He is accompanied by a son who is not our son, but he's our son. We welcome him. Baba says I should greet you. On the table, we have drinks, schnapps, soft drinks and beer. As if these are not enough, baba has supported the drinks with kola nut and money. These are for you. Sia gwa re! Is this not what you sent me? Everyone responded 'Eeeh.' Baba then interjected;

'We we won. Udova wen!'

'Oga osho!'

'Oga osho!'

'Ohoro oyen si vwo.'

There followed an outburst of laughter, creating a mood of merry making. It was now our turn to receive the drinks. Because we were considered to be 'book people,' one of the boys in the sitting was called upon to receive the drinks on our behalf. He went through calling our praise names and finally accepted the drinks. The kola nut was passed to Bojor's father who blessed and broke it. He then called each one of us one after the other. Whoever he called knelt down to receive his blessing and a lobe of kola nut. When it came to my turn, I easily did every thing right. This earned me praise from the assembly. The drinks were opened and served and soon it was a mini party. When we could have some conversation, I asked Bojor if this was how he was received anytime he came home.

'No, at least, not by my father. My father has made it elaborate to honour you. You see this is a custom that displays the openness, with which you were received. After this you'll feel free to come here anytime.'

Looking back now, those words came to have added significance. At the time Bojor said this, I wondered what on earth could bring me alone to this island, shut off from the dynamic tempo of life in the city.

Soon most of the men left. Gradually, Baba wore a thoughtful expression on his face. Gone was the boisterous mood that dominated our first contact. He was actually pensive. He stretched himself out on the throne, like someone looking for an opportunity to catch a snooze, and shut his eyes. In the comfortable silence that followed, Baba's voice rang out:

'Otadeferua,' he said. 'It's been a long day for me. I'm tired, and should go and rest. But I don't believe that what can be done today should be postponed till tomorrow.' He paused, regained his breath and continued. 'Every day we see new things. Some of them are good for us. Some need to be attacked. I'm sure you have heard all the noise about oil or no oil. God knows that in ordinary circumstances, everyone would have welcomed Shell ZP to our little community but the people are asking questions about the effects of exploration. They are asking what will happen after the exploration activities; are we going to eat dead fish like our brothers on the island? Are we going to have flames perpetually in our midst, drying up the little crops which we plant here? These are some of the questions we want the Shell ZP people to answer. Rather than answer us they are talking about security.'

'Whose security?' I asked rather naively.

'Security of the nation,' they said.

'We produced a document, which we wanted to use as a basis for an agreement and they accused us of being used by radicals.'

'We want them to state clearly that they will commit 20% of whatever they derive from our land to its development. But they say that it is premature to go into such an agreement. In the end, the meeting was adjourned till next month. We'll go there again to spend time arguing over little things.'

'I think you should stick to your point,' Bojor said. 'Right now, international opinion and national feelings are in your favour. Publicize your activities as much as possible...'

'That is the problem,' Baba cut in. 'No one gets to know about our plight until we protest. As long as they suck the life from under our earth and make millions of dollars, we do not make news. But once we say that they should compensate us for what they are taking from us, we become trouble-makers.'

I could see that Bojor was moved by the passionate way that this old man had presented the picture of the oppressor and the oppressed. This was not mere rhetoric. It was real. The lives of people were involved. The oppressor was no longer a detached, far away person whose activities we read about in radical literature. For the first time, I came face to face with the people who produced the wealth with which the Federal capital had been built. Whereas they did not even have surfaced roads, the wealth produced from the belly of their ancestral home was used to develop big cities, known around the world. Circumstances, I thought, can make radicals out of otherwise pliant gentlemen. It would seem that while I was reflecting on the situation, Baba had been speaking. I only caught what turned out to be the concluding part of his speech:

'...and the sad fact is that some of our sons sit with representatives of Shell ZP as directors, trying zealously to persuade us to accept explanations without an agreement. True is the proverb that man's foe is from home. Well, I think this is enough for one day,' he said rising so slowly from his seat.

We both rose too. He looked up and said, 'young man, I hope you will enjoy your stay here. So, don't let us blacken your mood with talk about black gold.'

'No sir. I ...'

'I understand. Go and sleep in peace.' He went into an inner room while we went to ours in preparation for the night. When Baba talked about black gold blackening my mood, I wanted to tell him that I supported his every move. I wanted tell him that no man is powerful enough to permanently intimidate a whole tribe or race or nation. That one must continue to struggle and fight for the improvement of one's immediate environment, that being the only way to guarantee a stable life for one's children and grandchildren. But for some strange reason, my tongue stayed glued to the roof of my mouth.

The voice of Bojor brought me back out of my reverie. 'The burdens we have to bear have children and grandchildren.'

I said nothing in reply, weighed by the enormity of the task before us.

When we entered our room, two large bowls were on the centre table, along with a little dish neatly covered with a transparent dish cover. Bojor gave a large laugh and seemed to get out of the depressive mood that fell on us after the encounter with Baba. He opened the dishes and exclaimed 'it's nice to be home.' Inside one of the dishes, were steaming pieces of boiled yam and plantain. In the other dish was fish pepper soup, spiced with local ingredients, which added a pungent smell to the soup. The third small dish was for palm oil. We had a good time. At the end of the meal, Bojor casually dragged out a gourd of palm wine under his bed.

'When did you arrange for all this?' I exclaimed in pleasant surprise. Well, I needed the intoxicating effect of fresh palm wine to lift the feeling of oppression that the encounter with Baba brought over me. Slowly, I regained my spirits. Slowly too I began to feel drowsy. When I stretched out my hand again to pick up the glass for more palm wine it was day. Bojor was not in the room. In fact, my hand had hit the wall because I was lying on my bed.

When I fully gained consciousness, I took a look around the room and guessed that Bojor must have woken up earlier to catch his father for an early morning talk. My eyes caught a hurriedly scribbled note: 'City boy, relax. Off to see the old man. Amuse yourself with palm wine. Signed, Bojor.'

More palm wine indeed! I had had enough of that stuff. Rather than immerse myself in the spirit of liquor, I put on my shirt and wandered off into the streets, with the sole purpose of seeing what the early morning looked like on a real island.

Even as I tread through this land of gold
I see nothing but dust and poverty.

It was quite early when I set out. I had left my 'ago Japani' (Japanese wrist watch as Bojor used to tease me with those disposable wristwatches which I bought) back in the city. Here in the village, one lost all consciousness of structured time. I met men going to the river to fish. Some men were obviously going to the farm. The children were not left out. They chattered like birds in the cool silence of the morning. Greetings filled the air. I walked on in the knowledge that the dark morning provided cover for any identity. I didn't want to be dragged into greeting people I didn't know from Adam. While walking with Bojor, it was alright, because I had a homeboy with me. I didn't mean this in a derogatory sense but in the sense that a companion who was familiar with the ways of the people served as my staff and shield. Those I walked past without greeting must have wondered about the lonely figure walking like a zombie, with his hands in his pockets

I wanted to think, and think clearly without bothering about who was walking beside or in front of me. I got to the end of the town and encountered the river, the gateway to the Atlantic. I saw the mist before I saw the river. In fact but for the shrubs that separated the river form the path, I could have encountered the bank without knowing that I had reached the waters of Obako River. The mist reminded me of Burutu, the village where I was born, while father worked with UAC, the forerunners of British colonisation of my country. Burutu, where I had my first encounter with education.

* * *

School was a four-block affair, fenced around by barbed wires meant to instil fear and dread in us as pupils. Anyone who ventured out of the barbed wire fence before closing time was never spared Mr. Obiebi's sharp strokes of the cane. The school shared a common boundary with a river, which of course meant that pupils were tempted to go for a swim, particularly during break time. As a result, a stiff law was imposed on all of us. Anyone caught near the river was flogged and sent on suspension for two weeks. Anyone who was actually caught swimming was sent out of school completely.

   Although there were strong reasons for this, some of my classmates grumbled bitterly at this unnecessary restriction placed on them. When I said that the teachers had enough reason to restrict us, I had in mind an incident that occurred before I came into the school. All teachers were familiar with the story and never failed to impress on us that they did not want wailing parents to welcome them home from work daily.

* * *

It happened long ago. A boy in primary two had left school in company of his classmates for the burial ground, a few metres from the school. In fact, the main road in the village terminated at the burial ground. From the burial ground where they plucked some guava fruits, they wandered to the river for a swim. Preye, the name of the boy whose plight eventually brought the entire community into a standstill, was an only child. His parents had been married for nearly thirteen years before the boy came grudgingly into the world. This was after so many visits to the river goddess and her herbalist. When Preye was born, everyone thought that he was a girl. He was not handsome. He was beautiful. He was, in the common expression of the people, the apple of his mother's eye. Preye and his friends went off to swim. He went down the river and never came back. Rather than raise an alarm, the others scrambled for their uniforms and rushed back to school where they pretended that all was well. At the end of the day, everyone went back home, but not Preye. Shortly after school closed, Mama Preye started searching for her child. The whole village heard that Preye was missing. Once anyone said Preye, it was obvious that it was something sacred that was being talked about.

an only son never dies a natural death;
even the lizard's persistent nod is a portent.

By this time, Mama Preye had gone berserk. No one in her immediate vicinity slept that night. Anyone in her house who tried to go bed was accused of being the witch that attacked Preye. Preye became a spirit, a spirit of fear, of accusation, of caution, of doom.

The next morning, Mama Preye resumed with the teacher of the catholic school and sat at the gate singing songs like a demented being. She sent her child to school. Did she do anything wrong by that? Why should the teachers send her only child to the lands of spirit? Teachers showed sympathy. Preye's bag and books were found in the classroom, which meant that he did not take his books from school the previous day. Mama Preye got wilder. The teacher must have sold him off to some 'gbomo gbomo.' She accused the teachers, physically attacked any one of them who came near her. She peered into the faces of children searching for her precious Preye. Preye did not appear in their faces. He appeared as a floating mass of flesh the next day. When the fisherman who found his body brought it to the jetty, Mama Preye fell on her beloved son, carried him on her thighs and started singing lullabies to the open-eyed Preye. People shook their heads in sorrow. Another lunatic had arrived.

may we never be locked in the pit
which an only child digs.

Mama Preye never recovered. Till her death on the track of a train one hot afternoon, she kept returning to the school to look for Preye. Preye would return from the teacher's house. Preye would soon return from his father's place. Preye would soon return from the marketplace. Preye will…Preye…Preye…In her demented state, she looked like a monster from the depths of hell, with scattered long hair, and dark dirty skin. The monster attacked any teacher she saw, and they all avoided her insane teeth.

the insanity of a deprived mother is an everlasting

etch in the memory of the unannointed; not even the
pacification of a million popes can generate the old tree.

When I started school, Preye's story was one of the first subjects taught in Catholic School One. It put fear in us, a fear of the river as a place that could suck in a child and make its mother become insane. Yet the river had a very strong attraction for us. It beckoned on us daily to taste its crabs, shrimps and fish, which were caught with ease. Yet the threat of drowning hung over everyone, and we still enjoyed staying close to the river to enjoy the mist that hung over it every morning. Going to school, one encountered the river. At school one encountered it. Leaving home was no different. Yet we were barred from going near it. While for some the ban lasted during school hours, for me it was twenty-four hours as imposed by my dad. The fishes and mist are all gone now. The river is now wearing a coat of oil bought by the almighty dollars of Shell ZP.

it is not only our own nakedness that embarrasses us;
a kinsman gallivanting with nothing to hide his skinny
body makes us put our faces inside a calabash.

A fair-complexioned mammy water was emerging from the river. A mermaid. No. She was just a girl who had come to wash herself in the river. For the first time in this land of innocence, my loins stirred in want of contact with feminine flesh. The mermaid barely had her body covered with a flimsy wrapper that was soaked with water. She walked casually in my direction and greeted me in the traditional way. I could not reply. I was arrested by the freshness of her beauty and her skin. She repeated her greeting before I mumbled something. Laughing recklessly, she glided on, gradually leaving my view. I wandered on, seeing this figure in every tree, every boat, and every house that I encountered. When I held tree branches for support, I imagined that I was squeezing Mermaid's thighs. Because the day had broken, I saw other girls returning from the river. I searched for Mermaid but never saw her again until I left for the city. About an hour later when I got home, Bojor was waiting for me.

Men who courted mermaids always
came back home with bad stories.

Our second day in the village passed like the first. Baba was not in for most of the day. Wherever we went, my eyes roved, hoping to catch

40

a glimpse of Mermaid once again. But no luck! Mermaid was my imagination. About midday, Bojor suggested that we pay a visit to his grandmother. I was a bit uncomfortable. I had never had any dealings with a grandmother. I did not relate well to old people. In their presence I maintained a silence which stupefied me. I only spoke when spoken to. It was with some trepidation that I encountered the blind, white-haired old woman who sat in the midst of relics from the past – cowries, pennies, boxes, hoes, nets, and other junk.

As soon as we entered her room, Bojor greeted her in the traditional way.

'Vre do,' she answered casually.

I thought she did not recognize her grandson.

'Otadeferua,' she continued, 'when did you arrive?'

'Yesterday.'

'Welcome. How is the coast?'

'We are fine, Nene.'

'Who is with you, a friend?'

'Yes Nene.'

'Friend of the chief's son, you are welcome.'

'Thank you grandma,' I said uncertainly.

'Find seats for yourselves.'

At that moment a rat ran out of a hole as if to welcome the visitors. And from the side of the cupboard, a cat made a swift attack, pouncing on it with ease.

'Cats must always pounce on rats and rats must always run away from cats. Any rat that falls a victim to domestic cat is a victim of its stupidity.' As if she was still talking about cats and rats she asked about the ruler of the land and concluded:

'We must pray for the day when our rulers must be our brothers. A prayer that our brother or son should become a ruler is a selfish one. What if our son ceases to be a ruler? Do we return to slavery? So, it's better to always have rulers who see us as their brothers and sisters. That way, they will always greet us in the morning, and ask us in the evening how we fared during the day.' She picked a small bottle from the ground, groping before she found it and poured the stuff inside into her palm and licked twice, showing a stained tongue.

'You must come home more often, Ferua, before the tide carries you away.'

'Nene, I need to concentrate on my studies…'

'Yes, concentrate on your work. It is good. But do not forget your people because you are concentrating. A man who concentrates on work and forgets the people will soon have no one to welcome him when he returns home.'

'Yes Nene,

'Have you been properly fed?' As Bojor told me later, this was a question she never failed to ask. 'Come here!' Bojor moved to her and she felt his body with her thin bone-like fingers. 'You have enough flesh. It is not good for a man to have too much flesh. He should leave that for women. Come, sit down here.' She grabbed a seat beside her and Bojor sat down. Mother and child. I started gaining an insight into how close he could be to his grandmother.

'Ferua, go to Umuko and tell her to give you two bottles of minerals. Ssh!' She hushed, 'don't protest, you must take my drink. Akpeteshi is not good for a book man like you or else I would have made you swim in Sapele water today. Off you go!'

Bojor dashed off like a little boy and I was left alone with Granny.

'Friend of Dada Ferua, you must be from Oto Ughoton. Your tongue gives you away.'

'You are right, Nene,' I answered politely.

'Listen,' a change in her tone, 'it's not everything which the eyes see that the mouth can describe. When two friends go fishing and the tide sweeps one away, the other must come home and bear witness.'

'I don't understand Mama,' puzzled by the expression of pain on her face.

'You must not let the tide sweep you too. One sacrifice is enough for the mouth of a hungry god.'

I had nothing to say to her esoteric talk, which sounded puzzling to me.

'As humans we outlive tendrils, yet when we see a beautiful tendril with extraordinary odour, we are sad when sunset snuffs it out. Yet there is nothing we can do to stop a tendril which chooses to wither even before sunset.'

I began to have second thoughts about her state of mind. Although she was blind, her eyes were open and stared into mine like a wild cat. Do I see something like a tear fall off from the side of her face? No it must have been my imagination. At that moment, we heard footsteps coming and presently Bojor appeared.

'It took you such a long time. I thought that one of the Umuko's daughter had arrested you.'

'Nene, I'm not …'

'Are you not a man? Serve the drinks. Keep the third bottle here. Yes here. Those two are for you. When the next visitor comes, I'll have something for him. As for me, you know I've never touched water

42

mixed with plenty of sugar. It's past my drinking time, but because we do not know when the tides shall return, I'll drink with you. Look under my pillow and give me the bottle there.'

Bojor got up and promptly fetched a small bottle of schnapps, which he handed over to Nene. Grandma opened it and neatly took a swig, carefully gargling with it before she took a swallow. 'Good akpeteshi! It keeps the mind going. As long as you have a healthy mind, your body will never complain.' I noted her philosophy and wished I could apply it some day.

'When are you going back? Tomorrow?' she answered before Bojor could reply. 'Yes, you always leave tomorrow. You come to see me when its tomorrow you want to leave. I like your consistency. May you go well.'

'Migwo ma.'

'Vre, omo me.'

'Migwo Nene,' I intoned.

'Vre do. You must come back to see me, even if your friend fails to come. Do you hear me?'

'Yes Nene.'

We discussed other things without any substance. Soon, it was time to leave. We stood up. She said nothing. Bojor repeated his intention to leave. 'Bye my son.' She just kept staring into space, taking swigs of akpeteshi as we left the room. When we got to the threshold, we both heard her say: 'A farmer who cannot make use of his hoe to harvest his crop, what does he need a hoe for?'

'Nene,' commented Bojor, 'just like her to wax philosophically anytime she takes akpeteshi.'

i hear a voice from the other side; a poet's voice
lost in the bleating of the captured goats.

When we left Grandmama, Bojor suggested that we pay a visit to the head of the clan, a grand old man of eighty years. He was not a king. But by virtue of his age and experience, all judicial matters revolved round him. His integrity was legendary, having been known to preside over all matters including those that included members of his family. At his place, we encountered a formal court session. In fact, he was summing up on the last matter:

'We do not encourage families to split; as much as possible a wife should stay in her husband's house to take care of her children. But if the family she is married to threatens her life, we have no option than

to allow her to go home and stay with her people until her husband is ready for her. Urhobo wado!'

'Eeh!'

'Sia- gware!'

'E yee!'

The family whose matter had just been looked into stood up to leave and a spokesman announced the next case. It had to do with a father and his son. Chief Okpako addressed the small assembly:

'Imoni Ofemu, an elder in this community has brought a case before us. It is unusual because it has to do with his son.'

'Let's hear the matter.'

'Ofemu will state the matter himself.'

An old man of about seventy stood up before the gathering, cleared his voice and began. First he greeted the assembly acknowledging both those he was older than and those who were older than he was.

'My brothers, I do not have much to say. Ordinarily, if my own son offends me, I would handle him myself. I would not come to this assembly, not because I do not respect you, but because some family matters are best handled quietly. Besides, all of you know me. In my younger days, no one could spite me and go without a sound slap. But on this matter, I have decided to bring it to the open because I have noticed that our sons are beginning to dig our graves while we are yet alive.' There was a pin-drop silence as the old man went on. All the banter and jokes had disappeared. The complainant did not raise his voice. He spoke softly but firmly.

'I want you to see for yourself, hear for yourself and tell us whether I have done wrong. As you can see, I do not have long to live; I am fighting for those who will be around to enjoy the land. I want my children to live in harmony after I am gone'

'Ofemu, your words are too heavy. You are not going to die. Remember that I your senior, I am still alive.'

'I know. May God give all of us long life.'

'You will live long.'

'I have lived long enough. Our people say that if one remains too long inside the pit latrine, he would be visited by all kinds of flies. I want you to judge between my son and I. As some of you know, I inherited nothing from my father. I laboured for everything that I own today from scratch. The rubber plantation, the garri factory came from my sweat; with proceeds from these, I have trained all my children who have the head for book. Five years ago, I called Akpomudje, my first son, and told him. 'I am old. Please manage the plantation for me and let's share profits annually. He agreed. He even promised to take over payment of the school fees of some of his younger ones. Since then, I have not seen a kobo; I have not received anything from Akpomudje. I have called him several times to find out what is going on. He gives me excuses or avoids me completely. His brothers complain but he ignores them. Is he right to control and spend my resources while I am alive, without consulting me? This is the matter. He is here. He has bought big cars and married many more wives. He has built houses for all his wives. Ask him if I have lied against him.' Silence followed, thick enough to envelop everybody. Finally, Chief Okpako coughed and broke the silence.

'Akpomudje! You have heard your father. What do you have to say about what he has said?'

'Ekpako me, Migwo! I greet you. My father for whom I have the greatest respect cannot lie against me. All what he has said is true. But let me explain something. As the first born, I have been managing the plantation. It is true that I have not given money to my father since I started. But I have given money to my brothers.'

'It's a lie.'

'Whom did you give money to?'

'Oji.'

All of these came from some young men sitting near the Chief.

'Silence,' a voice bellowed. 'We listen to one person at a time, and no one should call another a thief. You may continue, Akpomudje.'

'I've also used the money to create capital which I will use to develop the family land in Warri. They should be a little patient with me and everyone will smile.'

'Akpomudje, do-oh! Do-oh! You have spoken well. You have spoken as well as your sense can carry you. Because a child does not understand the world, he washes only his tummy while taking a bath. It is not day that comes to meet night. It is not night that comes to meet day. They both meet at the junction of life.' He stopped for a while, consulted with two men seated with him and continued. 'Your father did well by asking you to manage the plantation. Did he say that you should spend the profits without consulting him?'

There was no reply from Akpomudje. Chief went on:

'Do you have nothing to say? Why do you stare into the air as if you are expecting an answer from God?'

By this time, drops of water were dripping from the body of the accused. His big body started to shrink as everyone made sounds of disapproval. I really felt sorry for the thief.

'Akpomudje, is your tongue tied to the roof of your mouth? Have you suddenly become dumb?' an elder asked him.

'We pray that we do not see things that will turn us blind in our time.'

'Yes. When a son tills his father's land, the family land and gives out peanuts to the legitimate owner of the property, the world goes upside down.'

Ofemu sprang to his feet, and took the gathering by surprise.

'Akpomudje, do you see how you have disgraced yourself? Our people say that when death comes calling, a dog will ignore its master's whistle. Can you see your selfishness now? Imoni, the point has been made. Not even his mother could persuade him to change his mind before now. In the presence of everyone, I am taking back everything that I have given Akpomudje. If I ever see him in that plantation again, I will kill him with my last strength and follow him immediately. I thank you.'

The old man turned abruptly and moved towards the door. It took Chief Okpako some time to realise that the old man was actually leaving the venue.

'Ofemu, come back. We have not concluded the matter.' The old man was gone. The chief however went on to give the verdict of the elders. 'Return everything to your father and make peace with your brothers and sisters. Report here in the next edijana and let us hear how you have been able to pacify your angry father. The curse of an aggrieved father can ruin your whole life.'

* * *

We walked back into the street. For a long while, Bojor and I walked side by side without saying a word to each other. We did not even stay to see the Chief anymore. Later, Bojor muttered 'our people are beginning to learn the ways of the oppressor.' It did not make sense to me why a young man would appropriate his father's property and ignore all his entreaties for a fair sharing of proceeds. I said as much to my friend, who then replied: 'Ask our big masters in Abuja.' I said nothing after that. As a diversion I kept looking at both sides of the road for Mermaid to appear. Suddenly a thought occurred to me.

'Bojor, what was that joke about somebody's daughter arresting you?' I asked.

'Nene is fond of teasing me. She makes it a point to send me to Umuko's place to buy drinks anytime I come visiting in the hope that one of them would catch me and retain me as a husband in the village. To put it in her words, 'that is the only way she can keep me alive.'

I burst into laughter, much to Bojor's consternation.

'What's funny?'

'To be kept alive by one of those damsels is not a bad idea. I would be glad to change crosses with you.'

'Well, this cross is not for me. You can choose to remain here the rest of your life and write poetry in the bosom of a village beau. When the juice dries up, I suppose you'll head back to the city.'

Just like Bojor. He never enjoyed jokes about sex, marriage and women even though he relished the intimate company of a beautiful woman. The only joke he allowed himself to make was that he could never say no to a beautiful woman. He believed passionately that one must be committed to a cause. He was an artist to the core yet in the matters of the opposite sex, he avoided any conversation that tended to, to use his own words, denigrate the natural contribution of women to the struggle for emancipation. Once he lectured me:

'The first act of freedom ever experienced by man is through the woman. After being in the womb for nine uncertain months, protected by natural chords and vibrations, man comes into the world to face his challenges. The birth process is an act of freedom. It sends the child's spirit into the world as if to say: "enjoy the abundance of joy and misery in the world."

Although I didn't agree with him, I had nodded, hoping he would continue. But he had changed the topic into something, which I cannot remember now.

* * *

Early in the evening, Bojor took leave of me to see his mother. I stayed in bed, staring at the ceiling and ruminating on why Nene chose to speak to me in abstract terms. I tried not to pursue this too far because Bojor had said that Nene had a penchant for philosophical ramblings once she started on alcohol. But the words! On the wall, a wall gecko was trying to catch a spider, which itself had set its trap for an ant. While the spider was watching the ant, the wall gecko raised its head, at a good distance, waiting to pounce on the spider. I could not help wondering whether this was also the fate of man. Later that evening, shortly before Bojor returned, I wrote a poem:

> i a silent watchman
> of mother's heritage
> upstream spirit
> in turbulent seas
> what can you say?

the returning pestle
must slaughter
missed target now
powder after dance

yet visions shine forth
tied to strings of hope
and songs of tomorrow

Although it has since been redone, I still have the original drafts in my drawer at the moment. It is a seed in my memory of the pleasant days in Orereame.

When Bojor returned from his mother's place, he was full of spirit. He joked about Nene, about Baba's new revolutionary spirit.

'I find it amusing,' he said, 'while the flame of socialist international is running down worldwide, a revolutionary rebel is bred in the remote areas of the delta. To think that this man is nearly seventy-one years old.' Seventy-one years old! He didn't look a day older than fifty.

The rest of the night went in a hush. Baba returned late, by which time, palm wine and a meal of ripe plantain (onuko), usin (starch), eba, and bean soup had given me a technical knock out. I didn't participate in Bojor's conference with his father that evening. Just as well. Father and son needed to be alone sometimes. Later in the night, I dreamily noticed Bojor join me in the room. He mumbled something from his second mouth, slapped Mermaid on the back and crashed on the bed.

3

The hills of Obako beckoned on three poets in search of silence for inspiration. Far away, down the slope, where the feet of the high hill met with the road, and rays of different colours rolled by. These were ants to the vision of the elevated poet sitting atop the rock, taking breath, and trudging on in the hope of locating the comfortable bosom of the giant Panda. Bojor led the search, wearing a compelling seriousness on his face as if to impress on doubting Thomases that this was the journey so spoken by the dream of dreams. The dream of the redeemer cast high on the scaffolding of nature, facilitated by the rich sweet freshness of luscious palm wine.

Of course it was a journey into sweet confines of the unknown, the twilight zone that made the poet and his companions adventurers into the sacred warmth of nature. Nothing was definite; nothing was specific, yet they all wanted something, that thing which the rough-and-tumble of city life did not provide. It was also possible that the adventurers wanted the excuse of the hills to commit sacrilege. And they all rose up to dance. Questions kept coming to the mind of the wary poet. What dance was going to follow? A dance of death or a dance of hope? Or a dance of mystical unions, which would ferment the field of the future? We were going to see the wonders of the hills of Ekete, enveloped in the strong arms of huge rocks and boulders, and etched in the landscape by the force of nature. Later, Bojor told me that his encounter with the wholesome hills of Ekete gave him new notions of sacrifice. When I asked him how, he simply smiled and asked me to wait for his forthcoming volume of poetry. What a way of dodging the deep things while one enjoyed the beauty of the present!

A born-again zealot, once an active poet in the Writers' Workshop, provided companionship. She was in transition, on the fringe of experience, dancing between different opinions. When thoughts carried her here she did it with a fierce passion. At the other end, she also showed strong feeling. She was thus of many worlds, a woman of many colours. Without earrings, she still wore trousers that clutched her explosive body in a sensuous embrace. Her religion frowned at this. Her soul craved for it, and her poetry became the channel for rebellion against her father's religion. Eyes perpetually dreamy, what she lacked in facial beauty and intellect could be written on the top of a pin. It was her zeal that first caught my attention while Bojor gave the lecture in the remote private university in Ekete Land.

She was an organizer, a mover of people, and a persuasive speaker. Master of Ceremonies became a little tyrant compelling individuals to fish for and answer questions. She too was a bag of questions, a rainstorm let loose from an angry sky. How could Mary have given birth to God? How could Jesus have told a thief that he would be with him in paradise today when Jesus himself did not go to paradise that same day? Her questions always rankled everyone. On this day, all her questions almost poked narrow cleavages in the otherwise perfect lecture, which the Student's Association guest had given. 'Female Characters in the Works of Classical Writers' provided a fitting altar for the slaughter of male-controlled opinions. Contending that all the great female characters in classical drama were negative, Bojor argued that all through the ages, women had shown exceptional talent in manipulating the men who rule the world. Moji thanked the lecturer for pointing out this great defect in classical literature and then proceeded to ask what contemporary artists were doing to change the situation. It was a no-win argument that found a resolution in an extended talk at the Guest House.

At the Guest House, she was not as animated as she had been in the lecture hall. In fact, something seemed to have gone out of her, no spirit, no verve. I wondered what it was. Bojor tried to get into the spirit of the lecture, but everyone suddenly became self-conscious, withdrawn. The Head of Department, a headmaster of sorts, stood at a good distance from everyone watching with hawkish interest. We later heard that he was the sort of fellow who made blighting comments on yearly assessments on issues as trivial as how long a conversation went on between a female student and a male lecturer. Later in his career, he was enveloped by a devastating scandal with female students that smashed his reputation to smithereens.

I cannot remember exactly how the discussion drifted to visiting the hills and groves of Ekete. But suddenly, Bojor started to talk about a grove so beautifully painted by the female poet. He said something about making it a memorial of his visit. It was to be a kind of pilgrimage to the world of poetic ancestors, now locked in the jaws of delicately balanced hills. I was curious. It would be fun visiting the hills for poetic inspiration. At this time, I noticed a girl, very ample in size, staring permanently into Bojor's eyes. As I came to know later, she had been at it for quite a while. Bojor then threw an open invitation to everybody within earshot: 'Let's pay a visit to the hills of Ekete.'

* * *

We set out, four of us for the famous hills. Bojor, Moji, Desola, and I went to see the wonders of the hills. Between the university and the hills, we shacked ourselves into a rickety vehicle that plied the route. When I complained about the condition of the vehicle, Bojor was quick to remind me about our commitment to the masses. Here we were, he said, riding with the peasantry, experiencing what they go through everyday. Was this not a way of training us for the task ahead?

'I have come to enjoy myself,' I said, 'not to plan or study the rudiments of a revolution.'

'Sometimes, I do not know where you stand. How can you reduce everything to trivialities?' Bojor sounded exasperated.

When we got to the foot of the hill, we converged under a tree. Moji took over and tried to locate the best route to the top. Before long, she found one and the climb began. Here and there we found traces of sacrifice. At the first intersection we got to, we saw a white garment group seated in holy silence. Heads bowed, they gave the picture of a crowd of defeated people clutching to a desperate hope provided by a leader. The man who sat in front had a wizened face, with a little goatee that smelt of dishonesty. While his followers remained bowed, and eyes closed, his eyes darted from one follower to the other, occasionally settling on one of the female refugees. The leader indeed had beautiful captives. The smell of incense pervaded the air. An eerie voice from the leader suddenly pierced the air and that was the cue for mass vibrations. Shouts of 'Salvation! Salvation!' Rent the air. Bojor urged us to move faster. In no time, we were at the top of the famous hills. I looked down and said to myself: 'I can now overcome the world.' It did not stop my legs from trembling terribly.

Moji provided snacks after we settled down. Palm wine flowed freely and the initial reservations showed by Desola melted. She was not a chatterbox. But her tongue ran the length and breadth of the evening. Later, it was a picnic of silence, each lost in his poetic thoughts, as paper became decorated with the beauty of emotive words. Desola wrote:

When you see the trees swing
Dancing like the body of a giant masquerade
When the smoothness of the evening
Becomes the paleness of night
Even the fears of yesterday surge
With another power
The power of the past connecting
With the actions of the day.

'Bad poetry,' I told her, sniffing for trouble. I did not know she was a poet too. 'Does poetry come so easily to you?'

'I do not know what you mean,' she replied, 'I just know that once I get into the right mood, poetry comes to me. I do not need any inspiration.'

'Perhaps that is why you lack depth. Poetry explores the deepest part of our emotions, of our feelings. We do not switch our feelings off and on, do we?'

'Poetry is a craft to me, not emotions. I string words together, wed them and make sure the union carries meaning and works.'

Perhaps her words inspired me. I got locked inside myself after this conversation. Eyes spoke and suddenly there was a natural mystique in the air. Moji and the visiting poet drifted from the mouth of the grove into its inner recesses, of the sanctuary of voyaging poets. No words were spoken. The mystic poet dissolved into water.

* * *

Later they came down to the grove, which they had come to originally on pilgrimage. The light was no longer there. The beauty had faded into the canvas of consummated poetic feelings expressed in desirous terms, repudiating in bewildering tears all the truths of chastity faithfully paraded before all who cared to see. The truth was that liberation was also the road to departure. It must never happen again. If Moji must, then it must be after the nuptials. So be it. As they all descended the facial slope, the toys were additional glistening objects of scientific discovery. The mystic poet had a kind of laughter and Moji's zeal was somewhat subdued.

Why did we go to the hills? Was it really an exploration of nature in order to create the beauty of art in naked essence? Was there a hidden desire to demystify the sanctity of chastity? Time is our friend when there is nothing at stake.

* * *

As Moji left us at the junction that led to her hostel, I could not help but feel sorry for our artist caught adrift in the boat of conflicting loyalties.

'I hope you enjoyed the pricknic?'

'The what?'

'The picnic, rotten revolutionary!'

* * *

The return journey from Bojor's village was not as long as the journey to it. The boat was more stable. The boatman had a sense of decorum, and treated all passengers with deference. 'Sir' and 'Ma' were used in every sentence he made, so that I had to take a second look at him to know whether it was all a mockery. Truth was written all over his face. He kept a cheerful countenance, and the silence in the boat as we sped showed that all the passengers were listening to the beautiful voice of the boatman.

On the return trip, I took a closer look at the vegetation and noticed that farming would not take place outside the islands. There were creeks quite all right, but at least this could only house fishing settlements. In the midst of the swamps, there were giant rigs in different spots with a lot of activity going on. The white figures were quite conspicuous against the dark, green background of the mangrove forests.

I took in all of this as we sped on just as I had taken a last look at the jetty at Bojor's village. All the children in Bojor's father's compound accompanied us. By my rough count, they were up to forty (though Bojor stubbornly refused to tell me the exact number). I wondered about a revolutionary poet who still felt uneasy with taking a census of the people. Some revolution indeed!

It was a great crowd that saw us off to the jetty. I felt touched by Bojor's father's gesture. The man had personally come to our room to see us that morning. He brought a carefully wrapped parcel and gave it to me as a present. In sheer joy, I wanted to open the parcel, but something in the air made me look at my friend and at his father. The message was unspoken but clear. It is impolite to open a parcel in the presence of the giver. I clumsily covered up my thoughtlessness by expressing effusive thanks. He went with us over to the jetty, his brigade of children leading the procession, with the little gifts we had been given borne by the children.

We boarded the boat. As we drifted off, a sea of faces and hands started waving good-bye, endless good-byes as if we were going away to return no more. As the village receded, I caught Bojor's eyes and thought they were flushed. His father also remained there for a long time, staring into space, strong, handsome and kind, like a natural tower built for the defence of innocence. I took a last glance at Orereame and this time, it looked like a beautiful, well planned city perched in the middle of an angry river.

* * *

We reached Tosafe before the sun started sitting directly on our heads. The porters fell over each other trying to secure luggage, which they would carry. It was so rough. At one point, I sharply rebuked one of them for being so rough with my bag. He looked at me queerly and said nothing. Later, I saw him whispering to a co-porter, and they both burst out laughing. I felt like a fool.

* * *

From the Tosafe Park, we boarded a bus that was to take us back to the capital. It was while we were on the journey that echoes of Bojor's father's lecture at Ekete came flooding my mind.

* * *

The bus rolled on like a troubled elephant, though the driver and his mate loudly assured everyone that in no time, it would gather speed and we would sleep away like babies. I wondered what the bus would become if its speed could lull us to sleep.

* * *

As we travelled on the road to the capital, I marvelled at the large expanse of land that lay between two villages and wondered what our country would become if all its resources were effectively channelled in a progressive direction. I thought about oil and a bitter taste came to my mouth. Was it a curse or a blessing? The bitterness that came to my mouth was deep in the hearts of so many deprived people who had lost their sources of livelihood to exploration activities. Some translated the anger into violence, destroying brothers and fellow sufferers in the struggle. Some destroyed boats and attacked the working white men who represented their bosses in the country. One of the things Bojor's father said that stuck in my mind, was something to the effect that even a snake does not consume its own. It often reminds me of the story of Tuoyo.

* * *

Tuoyo was a believer in the power of wealth. Born into a middle-class family, his early ambition centred on working with an oil-producing company that paid fat salaries. After university education, he attended different interviews, sent delegations, begged to get an offshore job as an accountant. A celebration followed. Soon, a personal house was built, followed by another for his aged father. Prosperity had indeed arrived.

When the conflict between the oil companies and the local communities started, he was swallowed by the violence. His father's funeral over, he was kidnapped by fighting revolutionaries as an emissary of the oil exploiters. A demand was made for an impossible ransom, which kept changing daily. Before long, word came that he had been killed. No burial. No last respects. His poor kids could not link their father's death with the peoples' struggle.

Won't the ancestors get angry with the boys for killing their own while fighting against an external enemy? Was Tuoyo an enemy to the cause?

Sometimes, dog eats dog.

Years later, I visited his wife in the mansion that Tuoyo's blood built. She was a madam in the empire, taking solace in the romantic arms of a visiting pastor.

Pimps sit at the wheel of the nation's destiny, puny in wisdom, and gargantuan in arrogance and brazen display of power.

Giant oil pipelines that carried life away from their lands, bringing them peanuts in terms of jobs for unskilled labour, were now gradually decimating the quiet, natural environment. Most of them employed as menial workers with whom the prospecting companies

55

had no direct link. They were employed by subsidiary companies that paid a third of what they got from the prospecting companies to the workers. Some big shots in the city got the contracts to hire workers. These city men were like distant supervisors, lords of the manor who fed fat on the poverty of their people. A few of the workers were employed directly by the oil companies and paid salaries that automatically distorted social relations in the area. These men were spoilt by over bloated salaries. They in turn became over bloated in their sense of self-importance. Before long, they provided the bridge that finally led to the collapse of all resistance in last Delta Rebels.

They look like monkeys in celestial robes, strutting about the place with misplaced confidence.

Within a stretch of hundred kilometres, the driver and his boy stopped over ten times to pour water into the radiator. The vehicle was indeed in bad shape. Looking at it, one was sure from the outset that it would be problematic. However we were compelled to board it because it was the turn of the driver to take passengers. The alternative would have been to wait for the next vehicle. When we weighed the option of having to wait indefinitely for more passengers to arrive, we decided to take a chance. While paying the fare I asked the conductor, 'ol' boy, you tink say this your motor go fit reach Sapele so?' He replied, 'Oga, abeg make you no take bad mouth take spoil our journey o.' A middle-aged man intervened.

'No problem. Na bodi naim old. The engine strong well well.'

'Your conductor must learn how to talk to people.' I told the driver.

'Make you no mind am oga, na small boy. Make una siddon. We go soon dey go,' he said.

They drive cars that will carry the dead bodies of their clan into the abyss of disgrace.
The roads on which they drive the aeroplanes have craters that can swallow an oilrig.

Twenty minutes after the journey commenced, we ran into trouble. The engine coughed and stalled. The driver showed the real stuff of which he was made. He tried to start the engine twice. It refused to kick. Then the conductor said:

'Na this two men bad mouth, naim dabaru the motor so.'

Bojor and I looked at each other and smiled.

'Look here conductor,' Bojor snapped, 'if this rotten bus cannot get to Sapele, better refund my money and let me get out of here.'

'Yes. Give me my money too,' I joined.

The conductor looked relaxed, unperturbed by the intensity of Bojor's anger.

'Look here you little monkey, if you monkey with me I will teach you the lesson of your life.'

'Oga take am easy. I no be monkey. My mama dey sell garri for Tosafe market. Abi you don see where monkey mama dey sell garri for market?'

The other passengers found this funny and laughed. It was as if they could not see what was so clear to us. The driver then tried to start the bus again. This time the engine started emitting dark smoke. Everyone scrambled out. The passengers were divided. Some wanted their money back while others were willing to wait for the engine to be fixed. When we saw that all our efforts would amount to a waste of time, we carried our bags and got ready to leave. Finally, the driver reluctantly agreed to part with half of what we had paid as fares. At that moment, I suggested this to Bojor and he agreed that we should spend the rest of the night in Sapele. This was what took us to my uncle's house.

God punish them and uproot their ancestors from their graves.

Sapele was still some thirty kilometres from where the vehicle broke down, so we had to get another vehicle to take us to our temporary destination. Bojor was contemplative, particularly after his outburst and the complacent reaction of co-passengers.

'Education is very important,' he said, 'for people to be free, they have to be educated!'

'But how can they be educated if they are not free, if the circumstances do not make it possible for them to go to school?' I asked.

'The chicken and the egg dilemma,' he said tersely.

Just then a brightly painted jalopy waddled into a stop behind our broken down vehicle. Its seats looked recently refurbished, just like the driver who spoke impeccable English. Bojor negotiated the fare with him while I inspected the tyres. We boarded the car more because of the driver's apparent sophistication than for the roadworthiness of the vehicle. In any case, we didn't have a choice. New tyres were out of reach. Second hand tyres, popularly referred to as 'Tokunbos' that didn't last for more than one month of constant use, usually saved the day. And destroyed lives as well.

'But you know the risk in using worn tyres?'

'I know. I am a Physics graduate. I know it all. The situation on ground makes me put my knowledge in my pocket.' There was a lot of emphasis on the word 'Physics,' perhaps to underscore the importance of his discipline.

'So why are you a cab driver?' I asked, already envisaging the answer he would give. He looked at me as if I was a total stranger to the country.

'Do you really mean that question?'

'Yes of course. Why don't you teach Physics in a secondary school?'

'And stay three months without salary? And face the wrath of unforgiving dependants and landlords? It's better to give dignity of labour to cab driving than to lose the dignity of my certificate in front of an illiterate and greedy landlord.'

We did not say much after that. The cab just kept rolling on and on. It was a wagon. Bojor and I sat in the back seat. The driver kept stopping whenever he saw a potential passenger. When I asked him where he wanted to put the passenger, he indicated the tiny space between Bojor and I.

'It's the extra passenger's fare that we will use to settle the police.'

Logical, perfectly logical, I thought. Since policemen always on the road must take bribes (settlement they called it) drivers must look for their own ingenious means to raise the settlement fees.

* * *

As the vehicle rolled on, flashes of the discussions I had with Bojor in the first night came to me. I had thought I passed out after soaking myself in palm wine. I recalled now that that night Bojor told me the story of his childhood.

* * *

Bojor became aware of his status, his environment at the age of three. Early, too early, he became aware that he was the first male child, the only boy, particularly when playing with his mates. He was given almost anything he asked for. Before long, he became spoilt, yet no one could give him a spanking, knowing how it took a heir to spring from the loins of Orereame.

'That I managed to go to school and make it was a miracle, considering the amount of attention I got from everyone at home. The whole family would come crawling around me if I as much as complained of a headache. It didn't matter how many times of the day I feigned it. Soon I got bored with it all.'

School became a challenge where he had to prove to everyone that he was special. Luckily he had a naturally brilliant mind, a mind that could easily comprehend things, even complex information.

At the end of the first term, he came first in his class, something that became routine with him in the years to come. Teachers took a special liking to him and assured him that if he continued the way he did, he certainly would become a doctor. A doctor at that time was seen as the highest in the social order of things. It didn't matter what the interest of the child was.

Very early too, he became aware that his life had to be perfected. He was taken to different medicine men who made cuts on his body, and infused him with potions. Till he felt confident to get rid of it, there was a string tied to his ankle. This became a sure object of ridicule. When he moved to Government College, Warri he met sophisticated boys from Christian homes who wasted no time in making him miserable by constant reference to the bush boy from Orereame. Bojor could hold his own but until he shed the village toga, he was just another fortunate villager. When he returned home after the first term, he fought everyone. His father refused to budge. Throughout the holiday, Bojor fought a battle that he knew he had to win in order to feel wanted back at school.

He was still in this dilemma when the day to return to school came. He boarded the boat, waved everyone goodbye. Just before the boat berthed in Warri, Bojor took out the string from his ankle and threw it into the river. He became free. When he got to school, he walked about so confidently that in no time, everyone knew that a new Bojor had been born.

Bojor always led the class. One thing that amazed his classmates was his informal approach to reading. He never read beyond prep time. While his classmates stole from the hostel to practice what they called 'awoko,' he promptly went to bed and woke up very late the next morning. His notes were never up to date. In class, he would listen to the teachers with only one ear. He usually reserved the other for the novel he was reading, tucked under his notebook. Yet at the end of the term, he would top the class in all subjects. In the final exams, he cleared all his papers at Distinction level. Scholarship offers came. Everyone wanted him to be a medical doctor. When he announced to everyone that he would read Creative Arts, the general opinion was that a genius was about to fritter his immense talents away.

He became bohemian when he joined the Creative Arts Department of the Federal University, Jos. He threw himself into the theatre, writing plays, poems and short stories. He competed with English major students in their courses and beat them flat.

No one was surprised when he was awarded a first class degree in Creative Arts. He clinched virtually all the prizes in the faculty. He dazzled everyone by his humility, and self-deprecating remarks. In the valedictory speech that he gave, he extolled the spirit of commitment to intellectual ideals shown by lecturers, and called for a reciprocal gesture from the government. Concluding, he said:

'No nation, no matter how much it despises the liberal tenets of education, can afford to stifle minds by starving tertiary institutions of funds, or by comparing academics with civil servants. By the very nature of their training, academics are not civil servants; the university is not a Ministry. Except this fact is taken into consideration when making plans for our universities, the future generation will curse us.'

The resounding applause that followed the speech showed that he had struck the right chord. It was not only what he said that mattered, but also the way he said it. He said it to the right audience too, because the number two man in the nation's junta was present.

Youth Service took Bojor to Sokoto state where he served with the Television Authority. However, he spent most of his free time in the university where he met all kinds of foreign nationals. He was involved in the production of Shakespeare's Richard II, a play he passionately involved himself in because of its loud comment on dictatorship and power usurpation. At the end of National service, he came to Lagos to do a post-graduate programme in English. It was here I met him.

a small novel with a big story.

We got into Sapele town shortly before 3 p.m. When we arrived in Uncle Odiete's house, he was not in. But his wife was in and she gave us a warm reception. The children were all away to school and extra lessons. She showed us to the guestroom. As soon as my body touched the bed, I went out like a lamp.

4

Shortly after we settled in, Uncle Odiete returned from work, his hands fully occupied with the different items which he had bought. He was a boisterous old man, a man whose laughter could be heard three compounds away. His natural vivacity gave a wrong impression about his person, a mistake which none of his children, accustomed to his disciplinary measures even while smiling, never made. His cheerfulness had nothing to do with forgiving an erring child, nor tolerating his wife's sloppiness in carrying out her domestic functions. A wife's role in the scheme of things was defined and no woman, no matter how educated, could change things around him.

Apparently, the children had told him I was inside the house. Immediately he stepped in the veranda, he called out:

'Brume.'

'Yes Uncle,' I answered as I walked into the sitting room. Bojor was lying languidly on the bed as if he was replaying the events of the last two days on his mind. I met Uncle at the door.

'*Migwo*!' I greeted.

'*Vre do.* How are you?'

'I'm fine, thank you. And you?'

'We thank God. Have you eaten?'

'Yes, auntie has taken care of us.'

'Us? You mean you have company? Don't tell me you have brought a girl home for introduction!'

'No, Uncle.'

'The vehemence with which you said 'No' smirks of …or are you not old enough to take a wife?

'Sorry. I didn't mean to…'

'It's okay. So, who is it?'

At this very time, Bojor emerged from the room, a smile on his black face. He already knew the man we had come to stay with, at least mentally. In fact, while telling Bojor about Uncle Odiete, I had expressed the hope that they would meet someday.

That stuff about marriage thoroughly embarrassed me because it was the least of my concerns. The first and only time I discussed marriage with Uncle Odiete was when he told me:

'Brume, soon you'll become a man. I have this advice for you. When you marry, do all you can to keep the relationship. Never think of polygamy. It is an evil thing,' he said. 'One woman, one problem. Two women, two problems.'

'I don't think…'

'Yes I know. If you have to remarry, it must be because the first marriage collapsed. Don't ever keep two wives.'

I thanked him for the advice and assured him that I would be the last person to practice polygyny.

'Uncle, this is Bojor. Bojor, meet my Uncle.'

'*Migwo*,' Bojor greeted.

'*Vre do*. How do you do?'

'How do you do, sir?'

'Sit down, gentleman. Obruche, please ask the Lagos men what kind of drink they would like to take. You are welcome.'

'Thank you, sir,' we chorused.

Earlier on, I had said Bojor already knew the man he hadn't met. True. I spent seven years in Uncle Odiete's house, seven years of domestic and formal education. During this time, I came to understand him more than his children could ever do. He had twelve surviving children, all by one woman.

> *and they asked her: how many children have you*
> *she answered: eleven surviving children*
> *how many have you lost?*
> *the ground has swallowed four of my children*

My mum used to tell me about her brother who was so bright and intelligent that in his days at school, he would use a shorter method to solve a complex mathematical problem, much to the discomfiture of the teacher. He led the class all year round, throughout his five years in the secondary school. For some strange reason, he could never pass any external exam, that is, any exam conducted by bodies outside the school. So it came to be that he failed all GCE, 'London Matric' as it was called. After he left school, he became a pupil teacher in the same school, though he did not have the full papers required to teach at that level. The years rolled by, and gradually, Uncle came to accept his fate as a failure.

His former students suggested to him that he should organize private lessons for the pupils interested in Mathematics, English, and Latin. It was while he was doing this that he encountered boys who later came to hold strategic positions in the nation's political and economic affairs. One of such was Mr. Obazan (MBE).

* * *

Mr. Obazan had been Uncle's private student for one year, taking lessons in Mathematics and English. At second attempt, he cleared his papers and disappeared out of Uncle's life.

In 1953, the African Rubber and Timber Company sent out a notice, calling on able-bodied men to come take up employment and make a career. Uncle was one of those who responded. A day to the interview, it came to Uncle's knowledge that the head of the Recruitment team was Mr. Obazan. He went to see his old student in the Guest House where he was lodged.

'Good evening.'

'How are you, Mr. Odiete?'

'I'm fine. And you?'

'Doing well. I must thank you for the role you played in my life. May God reward you!'

'Thanks for recalling the past. You see, I've come to see you about a little problem.'

'Yes, what is it?'

'You see, I'm due for the interview of tomorrow.'

'I see.'

'So I want you to know that I'm doing the qualifying exam. Please if there is anything you can do for me, I'd appreciate it.'

'Mr. Odiete, but for the closeness between us, I would have had you arrested for coming to…'

Uncle Odiete was dumbfounded. 'I meant nothing bad, nothing dishonest.'

'Get out of this room. Now!' A baffled and humiliated Uncle Odiete left the room. Next day, he wrote the exam. He was not short-listed.

Three years passed and Uncle Odiete was at another interview conducted by the same organisation in another town. Mr. Obazan was not on this panel. On the day of the interview, suddenly, Uncle heard his name. An expatriate came out.

'Yes, here I am.'

'Are you the same man who did our interview in Warri?'

'Yes.'

'Then why are you applying for this job?'

'Because I have no job.'

'No job? How come? You came first in that interview.'

'I didn't get any letter.'

'Are you sure?'

'Yes sir,' he then muttered under his breath:

'Really, I wonder what these monkeys want to do with merit.'

Again, the expatriate recommended Uncle Odiete for employment. He was employed.

* * *

In 1958, Uncle Odiete's wife was expecting his second child. She went into labour that night, and was taken to the hospital. The delivery was a difficult one. The baby came tumbling into the world about midday. Uncle went to the office later in the day. From the look which fellow Africans gave him, he smelt trouble. Just then, the supervisor, a hard core, British, stiff-necked boss appeared:

'Mr. Stalin, when did you start running a Communist camp in my office?'

'I beg your pardon,' Uncle stammered.

'I did not know that I have been harbouring a communist in my office?'

'I am not a communist…'

'Then what are these?' He let some pamphlets drop from his hand and land on the floor.

'I got them from…'

'That's it. You're fired. Leave this office, now.'

Shut up. You are just another memory.
Erasable.

Just then, overzealous security men materialized and marched Uncle Odiete out of the company's premises. Another victim of imperialist conflict!

* * *

Uncle Odiete finally joined the civil service after the nation's Independence in 1965. An Inspectorate Division for food crops was one of the promises the new leaders had made. As a result, the Inspectorate Division entrusted with ensuring that cash crop farmers were duly assisted was formed. Uncle Odiete joined this division and spent the rest of his active life in service.

Known for his uprightness, he was posted to tough spots, where he quickly earned widespread respect for fairness. He accumulated nothing, because it was not in his nature to suck the filth of rotten wealth. While the spirit of probity lasted, Uncle enjoyed promotion and recommendations. However, things changed and the civilian regime that succeeded the first did not have moral probity on its list of priorities. Uncle became a victim. He was sent to a dead-end section of the Inspectorate, where he was no longer visible. He was not promoted. Until he retired, he was a shining example of a diligent worker, though a failure in the eyes of the people around him.

His family had grown in size. He barely managed to live on his salary, supported by his wife who did petty trading.

Uncle Odiete was a disciplinarian to the core. I had to live with him shortly after the death of my father. The amiable joking middle-aged man who came for me after the funeral turned into a hard, strict and disciplined father-figure. Yet he was ever smiling, as if life was one big joke, which he alone knew of, and was willing to share with no one.

I joined the family and became fully integrated, in less than one month. During the period of getting acquainted, I came to realize that the entire family was governed by rules. For example, as children, we had an interest in hunting out lizards and killing them for sport. Some of us got slings, which we used to aim expertly at the poor creatures. The game was indeed a very exciting one, particularly when we introduced the novelty of promoting anyone who killed a lizard with the first shot. A red neck lizard gained the marksman a double promotion. In fact, it was during these expeditions that I came to know all the ranks in the Armed Forces. We were all recruits when we started, and gradually we moved up the ladder. I remember I became a General in the army of Lizard Hunters. The boys on the next street did not have any regard for my General's rank. A mere hunter of lizards, becoming a General!

We grew up with models that became an albatross.

One day we went on our usual expedition. One of us fired and missed his target and cracked the side mirror of a car crawling from the hunting ground. We took to our heels. Because we knew all the corners, we got home pretty fast, and pretended that we were good and diligent boys. My cousin, Marien, was suspicious. In no time, she ferreted the truth out of the youngest of my cousins. When uncle returned, cousin 'BBC' broadcast the news to him.

'Papa, Obruche, Brume, and the others damaged a man's car this morning.'

'What? Damaged a car?'

'Yes. They broke his mirror.'

'Obruche, is it true?'

No answer.

'Answer me,' he roared.

'Yes uncle! Yes Papa! No uncle!' in a discordant chorus.

Inside the house, he slipped his belt out of his waist. 'Lie down,' he ordered. Twelve neat strokes on my innocent buttocks. Uncle had a way of ensuring that each stroke landed on the same spot. No wild flogging. At the end of it, we were all writhing in pain, screaming our heads off. 'Get them water.' Marien was on hand to perform this ritual. She dashed out and returned with a jug filled with water. After a forced drink, all the sobs and heaving subsided. Water had power.

'Now listen. From now on, NO THROWING OF STONES! If you pick up a stone, you earn yourself six strokes of the cane. If you throw it, twelve. And if you destroy anything, you know what I can do to you. Off with you!

The laws did not change anything
You must learn to fly without wings

Sometimes we vented our anger on Marien for squealing to Uncle. At other times, she would hold us to ransom for some particular offence, and ask us to do her share of domestic chores, or else…Doing extra work was preferable to uncle's cane strokes. Sometimes after working for hours, she would still go ahead and tell on us. We found this infuriating. We could not take revenge on her because she was above board in all things. It was frustrating.

Uncle always inspected our books, paying particular attention to Mathematics. Apart from the lashing which we may have received from our teacher in school, we could get additional strokes of the cane from him if for any reason we did not get some sums right. It was worse if the failed sum was what he had taught us at home before.

Once, while inspecting our books, he found an error, committed by both teacher and pupil. I remember clearly that whereas I actually failed the question on the opposite of 'remember,' it was marked right. My uncle was furious, blaming a fall in the standard of education on my teacher. As if this was not bad enough, there was another word which I spelt correctly, but which he marked wrong.

'When you get to school, tell your teacher that I said he should correct the mistakes.'

I didn't respond.

'Did you hear what I said?'

'Yes, sir'

'If you return to this house without pointing out the error to your teacher, you'll be in trouble.'

'Yes, sir!'

All through the morning, I felt miserable. How could I tell my teacher that he was wrong? I told my friend Mensah.

'If you tell teacher, he will flog you.'

'And if I don't tell him, my uncle will peel the skin off my buttocks. I'm in trouble.'

'Why not change it yourself?'

'Uncle will catch me immediately. I can't fool him with that.'

I dragged my feet till after break that day. Somehow the excitement of playing football during break gave me some confidence, and I walked up to the roaring lion.

'Sir, my father said I …'

'What? Your father, who is your father?'

'I mean, my uncle said I should tell you that I got this wrong, but it was marked right.'

'What, you want to correct me?'

'No sir, it's my uncle'

'Your uncle? Go and meet him at home to teach you. Get out, out!'

His voice frightened me. It sounded like something that was going to crack. His eyes bulged out of his face, not just out of their sockets. Drops of spittle came out of the sides of his mouth as he screamed obscenities at me. He picked his cane as I picked up my bag and made a rush at me. But I managed to slip out of his reach. I headed for home, confused, angry and afraid.

'Brughoro is in his room.'

'Brughoro? What is he doing at home at this time?'

'He came back from school earlier than usual.'

'Why?'

'He said something about his teacher sending him away from school.'

'Brughoro!'

'Yes uncle.'

I lumbered into the room. Anytime uncle was angry, his voice became soft and firm. Underneath the calm, was a volcano waiting to explode.

'What are you doing at home?'

'Uncle, my teacher drove me out of the classroom when I pointed out the errors to him.'

'What?' he roared.

'What!' coming from older persons was getting too frequent for my liking.

' He almost flogged me.'

'I see.'

I didn't really know who uncle's rage was directed at –the teacher or I. After a few a minutes he calmed down and ordered.

'Tomorrow, go to school as usual. I'll be there to see him.'

* * *

Uncle and a man were exchanging blows. The place was dark, so I could not see the other man's face. He gave uncle a blow on his face. Uncle stopped for a while to nurse his wound. The man lifted his hands and started rejoicing. From his low position, uncle suddenly sprang like a lion and fell on the rejoicing man. The man was on the floor. Uncle was pounding him. He started bleeding. His head started dangling as if it would fall off. I ran into the ring to stop uncle from killing the man. He pushed me with one hand and flung me to the ground.

I woke up.

* * *

It was morning. As soon as I opened my eyes, bright morning light hit me. Somebody was tagging at my collar.

'Wake up. Don't you want to go school?'

I stood up, feeling angry. I staggered to the bathroom led by Marien. She poured a cupful of cold water on me and sleep disappeared. Gradually, it came to my conscious mind that I would be facing the teacher today. My heart raced up and climbed down. A bitter taste came to my mouth. I shivered a little. The breakfast of tea and bread tasted like ashes in my mouth.

'Brughoro, make sure you enter your classroom.'

'Yes uncle,' I answered, though I had no intention of obeying him.

* * *

When the bell was rung for the first lesson to commence, I was standing outside the classroom. After the morning assembly, I had waited outside for the teacher to come to the classroom. The cold stare which I got in response to my 'good morning sir,' confirmed my worst fears. The man had not forgotten about yesterday.

How could I have avoided the ugly situation I was in? Perhaps I should not have allowed my uncle to see the page. Stupid! Uncle would have gotten more suspicious. Perhaps I should have kept quiet about it with my teacher. Foolish! I would have incurred my uncle's wrath. I was in this state when uncle tapped me on the shoulder.

'Is this your classroom?'

'Yes sir.'

'Why are you not inside?'

No answer.

'Come with me.'

I tagged after uncle, wondering what would be the end of all this. Here was uncle looking resplendent in his starched Khaki uniform as an Inspector of Agricultural Produce. Behind me, in the classroom, the man whose voice and cane shaped my days was teaching my colleagues.

We got into the headmaster's office. It was a place no one went to except when there was trouble. I was surprised when the usually belligerent headmaster stood up and politely exchanged greetings with my uncle. The tension went down a little bit. I had thought a shouting match would ensue. Finally, uncle came round to the point, which had brought him to the school.

'…you see, I was surprised when I got home that day and met the boy sleeping.'

'Well such things happen. I think we can straighten all this. You, (this was to me) what's the name of your teacher?

'Mr. Ofan Ofuafo, sir.'

'Benson, go and call one Mr. Ofuafo from Primary Four B.'

'Yes sir,' the office boy responded.

> *Even if you said that your mother was a pig*
> *No one would believe you.*
> *If you said your mother's witchcraft killed*
> *Your father, they would copy it into the big book*

There was tension in the air as we waited for the teacher to come. A few moments later, he hurried in, looking and sounding polite to the headmaster and his visitor. When he saw me, the expression on his face changed slightly.

'Mr. Ofuafo.'

'Yes, sir.'

'Do you know this gentleman sitting in front of me?'

'No, sir. Good day, sir.'

'Good day to you,' uncle replied.

'That fellow there,' the headmaster said, pointing to me, 'is his son. Now, do you know him?'

'Yes I do. Brughoro is one of the best students in my class. I know him very well.'

'His father says that you sent him out of school yesterday, because he pointed out an error to you.'

'Did I send you out?'

I was surprised that Teacher had taken this line. I looked at the entrance to the office whether any of my classmates would walk in and support me. There was nobody. I imagined the wrath of teacher after father's departure.

'Eh... did I send you out? So you have joined the group of liars, eh so you have joined the bad boys?'

'No sir...you sent me....'

'Shut up, I did not send you out.'

'Now let us look at the notebook which he complained about,' the headmaster said.

I fished the notebook out of my bag, while the three adults looked on. When I handed it over to the headmaster, everything stood still. I wondered if my uncle was wrong. Would the headmaster take sides with Teacher? Would I be found guilty of some offence? The headmaster's face remained blank. He beckoned Teacher to come over. In silence and whispers, they looked at the page that caused the trouble.

'So you see, the boy's father was right.'

'Yes, I mean... sir... I...' Teacher stammered.

'Mr. Ofuafo, I have always advised you to be more careful. Do you know what damage you have done to the image of the school?'

'I am sorry sir, really sorry. It must have been marked right in error. I know that it happened when we exchanged answer sheets and asked pupils to...'

'Don't talk like a fool, please. I expect such exchanges to be supervised by the teacher.'

'You are right, completely right sir. I am sorry.'

'Are you sorry that you gave a wrong assessment or because you unjustly sent a pupil out of the classroom?'

'I swear in the name of my God in heaven, I did not send the boy out of the class.'

'Don't take the name of the Lord in vain,' my uncle cut in. 'It's enough to have punished a boy for delivering his father's message. Do not compound your problem by bringing blasphemy into this.'

'On behalf of my staff, I apologize for everything that happened. I will take steps to ensure that there is no recurrence of this type of behaviour,' the Headmaster said

'Thank you, Mr. Osiobe,' Uncle Odiete replied, rising from his seat.

All through this, no one seemed to have noticed my presence. No one invited me to testify against my teacher. It was a great relief to me when Teacher fell into step with Uncle Odiete as the latter stepped out of the office. He was really at pains to convince Uncle that he meant no harm. I was really amused that my teacher could tell such a barefaced lie. It was only later in life that I came to understand why Teacher lied. He wanted to protect his job.

In my country, the lies that our leaders tell are meant
to secure them against our fury. We must not know the
ugly truth about our leaders; or else we would
revolt and stone them as they drive along the streets.

When we got back to the classroom, he asked in a rather loud, belligerent tone:

'Children, did I send this boy out of the classroom?' There was no response, just silence, silence to show that they knew Teacher was lying and that they could not say it for fear of being punished later. Teacher understood this and played the game often. At break time, I knew that the boys were really pleased that Mr. Ofuafo had been cut to size. Looking back now, it was a challenge to the authority of my Teacher. Who was my uncle to tell a teacher that he was wrong? Later in life, I encountered different situations in which persons were compelled even in church to believe a lie, a fraud, and attribute it to the mysterious ways of God.

When the pastors lie, God does not strike them dead
Yet they tell us God will punish us for lie telling

'Religion, particularly Christianity provides an answer to all the problems of man,' Uncle Odiete was explaining to Bojor. 'It prescribes a wholesale cure to the ills that plague mankind.'

'That is the reason we must be cautious,' countered Bojor, 'any human institution that claims to have an answer to all human problems must be carefully examined.'

'That's where you are wrong. Christianity is not a human institution. It is a divine institution. God established it through His only begotten Son.'

'The leaders of the church, of Christianity, are they not human beings?'

'Of course they are.'

'Don't they make mistakes?'

'Yes they do. But that does not mean that Christianity is wrong.'

'The leaders of Christianity misled the world for ages. They committed a fundamental blunder when they used the Bible to justify slavery. Our race has not been able to get out of the quagmire.'

'The Bible does not support slavery. The white men who did so were racist Christians. Except they repent, God will punish them.'

'So you see how a few persons can discredit a race, a religion? Who do we hold responsible, the religion or the adherents?'

'Listen young man,' preached Uncle Odiete, getting more passionate as he spoke. I could see that he was barely controlling himself from slapping this impudent fellow who was challenging his authority right inside his house. 'The Bible is God's inspired word written by men of old.'

'Written by men?'

'Yes, written by men who were moved and guided by the Holy Spirit. They did not write their own ideas.'

'How can anyone prove that they did not write their own ideas?'

'Our faith in God tells us that they did not write down their own ideas. Some of them did not understand what they wrote. It became clear to them only after they had finished writing. So they could not have written down their ideas.'

'I do not see how this answers the question….'

'You are a heretic, young man,' declared Uncle Odiete in exasperation, 'there is nothing that I can say to change you. I suggest we stop this discussion here. May God forgive you.'

'I have nothing against God. I am only disenchanted with the way some so-called Ministers of religion play God and insult our intelligence.'

'Still, you are a heretic. I must be careful with you.'

'I'm not a heretic. I just want to know. I seek knowledge. You see, it is said that Christ died for us in atonement. Some others have contended that Christ did not complete his mission because he was meant to preach to the world, not to die for it.'

'There you are wrong again. Christ completed his mission. He said: 'It is finished.' Besides his death has helped to spread the Christian faith to the uttermost part of the earth.'

'Sacrificing one's life for others is a terrible way of making a point.'

"The Messiah's death was different. No matter what your heretic opinions are, the death has changed the world.'

'Yes, the same way Saro Wiwa's death has changed life in Ogoniland.'

'Will you shut up your foul tongue? Where did you pick this type of person for a friend?'

That was it. I wondered how Uncle was able to keep his temper while the dangerous conversation went on. In a way, I still had not overcome my reticence with him. I still could not bring myself to actually argue with him. In spite of the explosion, they seemed to enjoy each other's company. I suppose Uncle did not often get persons who could bandy words with him, who could challenge his rigidly held ideas. Bojor was a good change. On another occasion, I caught the end part of their argument. Uncle said:

'But sacrifice itself is a way of life. When we give up all that we have to ensure that others live, we are making a worthy sacrifice for which we shall be rewarded by God.'

'If there must be sacrifice, it must be an end itself, not a means to an end. If I sacrifice all my earnings on educating my children, it must be because education is good, not because I want them to provide for and fend for me when I am old.'

'Where do you get all your funny ideas from? Is there anything wrong with expecting one's children to fend for him when he is old?' asked Uncle.

'No, nothing except that it means one has made sacrifice for selfish reasons. In fact such an act is no longer an act of sacrifice. Sacrifice must be selfless.'

'I take it therefore that you are not opposed to the idea of sacrifice itself. What you are saying is that the bearer of a sacrificial burden should expect no reward.'

'Yes, in a way. But you see, we have seen too many cases of 'after all what I have done for you' to make one believe that sacrifice is ever selfless.'

Since we arrived in Sapele, Uncle Odiete and Bojor had argued on every topic under the sun. During such arguments, I kept quiet. In a way, I was happy that they met. It was interesting though that they never saw eye-to-eye on any subject. For instance on the issue of political leadership, uncle Odiete castigated politicians for messing up the affairs of the nation and praised the ruling junta for cleansing the putrefied political arena. Bojor took the other side and blamed the military for making itself an unregistered political party. In his view, the best military dictatorship was repressive and undemocratic. He also blamed them for putting fear into the minds of politicians and concluded that each time civilians were in power, they never stopped looking behind their shoulders, so that the soldiers will not take them by surprise.

We were in Sapele when the newspapers started reporting news about depositing toxic waste in the port town of Koko. The nation was shocked that such an affront on the collective dignity of the country could take place under the apparently watchful eyes of the military regime.

No doubt the soldiers were more interested
in watching over the vaults of the nation's Central Bank.

The vessel that brought in the nuclear waste had escaped the not very watchful eyes of the nation's security agencies. I remember the incident very clearly because the newspapers gave details about the danger of such toxic waste in any country. In exchange for some hundreds of thousands of naira, certain unscrupulous persons had allowed a ship bearing the waste products of a Western nation's nuclear reactors to the quiet and serene environment of Koko.

White man shit for Blackman country
Pope no vex for dat one?

Koko had always held a special fascination to me because of its natural port. In spite of the huge commercial activity in the town, it still managed to retain its beauty and tranquillity. In a way, the inhabitants themselves never enjoyed the economic benefits of the ports. The big business men from the major cities simply carted away goods which had been imported through the port and went somewhere else to enjoy the fruits of Koko port. When I said this to Bojor, he sarcastically replied that it was the typical national way of development. He added that all the effusions in the papers would end very soon and that all the national monkeys and their bloodsucking lackeys would ensure that the news died a natural death. I did not have cause to disbelieve him.

Even their mothers will not defend them
When the moon breaks out of the prison
Asaboro slept and did not wake up
No one shed a tear, not even his wife

We spent two days in Sapele. In those two days, I gained an insight into Uncle Odiete's personality more than I ever did in the nineteen years that spent with him as a boy. He held to his views rigidly but was bold enough to try them out in open discussions. He seemed to have moved with the times but in a traditional way. At the end of our stay, he promised to visit with us in the capital city before the end of the year. I did not take him seriously until he arrived late one July evening and magisterially sent for me. That is a future story. We left Sapele very early on the third day.

How shall it sound when it is reported that there was
Not a soul left to tell the story?

5

How does a man bear the burden of the knowledge of the impending death of his closest friend, revealed by no less a person than the friend's aged grandmother? When we walk along the streets, eat in the house, and laugh over politics, how do I successfully keep the turmoil of my heart from taking over the smoothness of my face? When we crack our usual jokes about women and fancies, I feel pained that this laughter would die if I speak grandmother's words to him. Sometimes, I am tempted to think that it is a betrayal of trust to hide the prophecy of the future from a friend. Yet I know that once he gets to know the prophecy, life may become a mere ritual, awaiting a fatal resolution of a lingering conflict.

> even if I sing the song of my ancestors
> *they will not let me go; the palm kernel*
> of the matter lies in the hands of the others.

This feeling of betrayal is highlighted any time my friend says 'When I am gone, is that the kind of interpretation you will give to my poems?' To keep things going, I retort: 'Why are you so sure that you will go before me'? Usually, there would be no answer.

Once I caught a glint in his eyes, which made me very uncomfortable. I must have given myself away some how because he asked me whether there was something I knew which he did not know about. I skilfully said something to the effect that he was being presumptuous thinking that he must know everything that I knew.

Alone I bear the burden, like the snail its shell.
Revelation of the truth can bring disaster.

The truth shall set you free, but it can make you squirm first.

It all came to me on our last night in Sapele. The dream about a fading firmament made it all clear to me. Initially, I thought it was my imagination. After the dream, Bojor's grandmother's statements became too clear to me. The star would shine forth and fade out in no time. Who can prevent a star from being bright? Which force also can stop it when it must fade? The star must shine to be recognized, but it must also fade to give way to another.

In a way therefore, I was not the only one with a burden in the heart. Grandmother had borne it for a long time before she decided to share it with me. But the weight of hers was light, because Bojor was always away, always in the 'coast' living an extremely active life. To me, each new day seemed to bring the end closer.

* * *

We arrived back in the city late in the afternoon, and ran into a heavy downpour. The major roads were all flooded and the car in which we were travelling had to swim through. Without rains, the roads were a beauty to look at and a luxury to drive on. At night, the roads were floodlit, making it unnecessary for drivers to make use of their headlights. There had been so much noise in the media about the road when it was built three years ago. It was declared the best road in Africa. Everyone believed the civil engineers who were supervising the road construction under a new programme created by the junta, called 'DIRECT AND INDIGENOUS LABOUR PROGRAMME.' Under this arrangement, there were to be no foreign engineers. Only citizens of the country were involved in designing and building the road. The road was like the beautiful bride who rejected all the suitors, but ended up in the house of the monster. That is, it was beautiful till the rains came. Everyone cursed the engineers. How could one build a road without a drainage system? The outrage from the Press after the first rains matched the praise and commendation that followed the success of the road project. In spite of the gag on the Press, an Editorial from *The Guideline* actually called for the sack of all the engineers in the Ministry. But the matter ended there and we are still saddled with the beautiful road without a drainage system.

And they sold the looms of their ancestors
For a mess of stinking pottage in a night's deal

We disembarked at the Central Park in the middle of the town. The flood was staring at us with a hungry expression on its face. Fortunately, we got on a bus that took us to the Youths' Hostel in Ariga. Built by the missionaries nearly sixty years ago, Youths' Hostel provided a resting place for all kinds of characters who had migrated to the capital city in search of a living. By all standards, the rate was cheap. Bojor and I went to our different rooms.

Our return coincided with the publication of Bojor's play, *Rooms and Rivers*, by a reputable publishing house in the country. We had a minor celebration, all of us -- Bojor, Ovigwe, Rasta Man, Shata and I. As usual, the lagoon front was our host. We freely drank palm wine, made jokes about everything. Rasta man was in high spirits.

'It is Providence that has opened your way. This is the opportunity we have all been waiting for. Now Bojor, above the sky is your limit. Do not look back, if you do, you no fit for the kingdom.'

'Six whole years,' mused Bojor, 'six whole years for the publisher to rouse himself from slumber. I had almost given up.'

'No. Your genius is like a calabash. It can't remain under water.'

'I suppose we don't get to know or meet all geniuses. What happens to a genius who grows up in a backward, illiterate society?' he asked.

'Somehow, the brightness of his mind will permeate his immediate environment. He may not be quoted in books, but some how, a record of his activities goes into communal history. This might be like the case of the lamp lit and put under a table. It may not light up the entire room, but it certainly will provide light for whoever wants to make use of the under table.'

'Don't you think that one should relocate if his immediate environment does not appreciate his worth?'

'And abandon the people he is expected to light a path for?'

'Not really. If his life is at risk, he should move to a place where it would be useful, where he can serve humanity.'

'You see, the Almighty has a way of sending supermen to areas of ignorance. It is the duty of such a man to lift people out of the depth of ignorance. The process entails patiently educating the people through courageous acts.'

'…and lose one's life in the process?'

'It is not life that matters,' retorted Bojor, 'but what you achieve with the life that you have. A thousand years of worthless living would amount to nothing if the individual concerned frittered away all his talents. There are some men in history who lived for only thirty-four years and through their actions, altered the thinking of mankind. The

People's Princess was barely 30 years old. But when she died of breast cancer, she brought world attention to the plight of cancer patients.'

'There is something sacrificial about the genius,' I chipped in. 'Most of them are eccentric in one form or the other. It's either they womanise, or they befriend the bottle. Some can't stand family. It's as if the talent of the genius must be put on leash by some peculiar predicament.'

'Perhaps,' Bojor cut in, perhaps it is nature's way of ensuring that a genius achieves high concentration. A genius without a focus who enjoys every other thing that men enjoy cannot achieve much. Geniuses usually are rebels.'

Ovigwe who had been silent all the time intervened at this point:

'What happens when two geniuses marry?'

'Explosions.'

'Not even through research collaboration?'

'Perhaps it is possible. If the search for knowledge unites two geniuses, then the union is an intellectual one. Marriage ties are secondary.'

'You imply that geniuses are one-dimensional. A man or woman who cannot enjoy the simple things of life cannot be said to be a man.'

'For such people,' Rasta said, 'their life is a special assignment. In a manner of speaking, they are emperors of their salvation. Their lives are a fixed equation. They are prisoners of their acute sense of what must be. Some go the way of self-destruction but in the process manifest the greatness of their mind.'

'We pray for husbands, not geniuses. If a man cannot be a husband, his ingenuity should be left in the other world,' Ovigwe said.

There was an electric silence in the air after this, a silence so deep that a person happening in on the scene would have felt it on his face. Ovigwe stretched herself on the branch of a fallen tree pretending to enjoy the moment. Her eyes looked withdrawn, her lips quivered. Genius and I moved to her. Her mind was a book open to the love of her life. Bojor read it aloud to me once, having chanced on the lines in her secret diary.

* * *

I love him, yes I love him, and I know I love him. I want to possess him, to make him possess me. I want him to enter my spirit just as I want to enter his spirit. Sometimes I try to enter him, but I run into walls of steel. I am still searching for the keys to unlock the gates. When he declares his love, it is sweet, but sometimes he brutally attacks what such declaration stands for. Is it an indirect hint that he intends to reign solely in his empire? At such times, I hold myself, I arrest my emotions, I do not want him to know how much I want to possess him. He knows that I love him. He knows that I would die for him, slave for him. Does he secretly despise me for it? Am I an impediment to his genius? Do I count in his reckoning? Perhaps I am being selfish trying to possess a man whose ideas can change the world. But I want a husband, a man to call my own, with whom I share some things, some ideas. I do not want a relationship with those fellows from my hometown who simply want a wife for baby rearing. Bojor is different, would be different. At least I think so. Those far-away looks sometimes scare me, though.

Yet when we are together, our spirits talk and we know that we both understand our insides. Then we both know we should listen to our insides and find that string of steel to hold on to. Yet we sit in front of the lagoon and denounce all that we should be doing. We discuss the revolution, and how the oppressors must be vanquished when our people come to power. We discuss the military in government and condemn all their atrocities. We condemn oppression of the minorities and think of ways of ensuring that minority rights are respected in the land. Bojor can't stand the sight of green anymore. So each time we are in front of nature, the military image comes to his mind. He swears at them with a rage that often shakes me. I seem to be at the receiving end. He does not touch me. He says he likes me pure, natural and that we must maintain reasonable diplomatic relations without commitment. But I know that he does things with the other ladies. The other day, G.G. said something like women being a tonic to the revolution. Is that all I can be? A tonic? I cannot understand it all.

The sweet wailing voice of Rasta purring from the other corner killed silence.

> If you cannot come
> I cannot go
> Can't do without you
> Can't be with you
> Yet I'll hold on

Bojor sprang from his reverie and proclaimed:
'Comrades, let us drink to the future of art in our country. Long live the writer.'
'Long live the writer,' we echoed.
'Long live the people.'

'We shall outlive the people.'
'We shall outlive the people.'
'Who then shall read our works?'
'Who then shall read our works?'
'The people shall read our works!'
'The people shall read our works!'
'Long live the writers.'
'Long live the people.'
'And long live Ovigwe.'
'Long live the women who make the hearts of men light.'
'Yes, to carry the heavy burdens of the world.'

* * *

Rooms and Rivers received good reviews in the papers, though Bojor was very cynical about most of them. He felt that most of the praises showered on the book were for the wrong reasons. He took particular exception to the reviewer who opined that the play "represents a scathing denunciation of the messiahs of Africa who have failed to learn from the lessons offered by the colonialists." Bojor threatened to bar the fellow who wrote such uninformed commentary for people to read from attending future performances. He practically ignored all the others who though said one or two uncomplimentary things, did not give a 'neo-colonialist interpretation.' He picked up his pen and drafted a rejoinder. After the first draft, he gave me a lecture:

'To classify me as an apologist for colonialism is the greatest insult that anyone can inflict on me, on my person. I regard the colonial encounter as the greatest act of racism after slavery.'

'Mr. Writer, I agree with you on a rejoinder. But remember that once a work of art travels into space, it is no longer the duty of the writer to explain. How many people do you intend to explain to?'

'I'll explain to the world. If I can access the mind of one person through my rejoinder, I'll would rest in peace.'

'Just be careful so that you are not accused of being intolerant of other people's views on your work.'

'Too much ignorance in the Art Desks, too much ignorance. I can bet that most of those boys do not understand the dialectics involved.'

'Dialectics? How much food does it bring to the table? How much money does it stash in your bank account?'

'Enough of your sarcasm!'

81

'Thank you. As for the other idea of barring an ignorant reporter, swallow it even before you vomit it. The 'soja' mentality seems to have caught up with you too. A shame…'

'I beg your pardon. Certain fundamentals must remain sacrosanct even in criticism. A critic without a sense of history cannot discharge his responsibilities both to himself and to his society.'

I read his rejoinder:

I consider it preposterous for any critic to suggest that our leaders ought to have learnt methods of administration from the colonials. Colonialism was as wicked as it was exploitative and our people may never recover this century from the harmful effects of that debilitating encounter. It's on the same level as slavery, that pernicious institution that uprooted millions from their native land and transported them to a hostile environment, where they were used as the fulcrum of American development.

* * *

It took two long weeks for the leading paper to publish the rejoinder.

Even if a pint sized man rapes a giantess
The colour of the crime remains the same

* * *

A week after we arrived from Warri, I had a visitor. Barrister Meka Ogbon a classmate of mine from secondary school descended from the sky one evening and brought boisterous laughter into my room. That evening we had just concluded our usual review of the newspaper reviews and was getting ready for dinner when Meka knocked on my door. It was great pleasure to see the great Meka after such a long time. He had been a very good friend, reliable, brilliant and aggressive in the quest for wealth. Judging by his appearance, he seemed to have hit big time. He was dressed in a complete black suit, red tie on a white background. In the language of the times, he looked corporate. His limp had reduced considerably in spite of the fact that he had stopped using the cane. His black shoes looked well polished, glistening and bright. They were a far cry from the shoes he used to wear in our school days. Then, he wore specially made shoes to help his disability.

'Man Meka,' I roared the way we used to call out while in school. 'Where did you shoot out from?'

'From the moon,' another round of laugher.

'This is Bojor,' I said, pointing at Bojor.

'I'm Meka Ogbon,' my friend announced, not waiting for me to complete the introduction. 'How are you?'

'I'm fine and you?'

'Coasting along, though I can't complain.'

'You are the first man to say I can't complain.'

'Really, you see I thank God for what he has done for me. I went into Maritime Law having been directed by my inner mind. Since then it's been boom!'

'Lucky you,' I said.

Just then Ovigwe entered.

'Hi everyone.' And she proceeded to give Bojor a peck. She was introduced to Meka.

'Pleased to meet you,' she said formally.

'Same,' Meka replied.

'I picked a review for The Star today, did you read it?' she asked Bojor.

'No. Do you have a copy?'

'Certainly. Here.' She handed over a copy to Bojor.

'What is that, if you may pardon my curiosity?' Meka asked.

'It's a review of Bojor's play.'

'Oh I see. When you introduced your friend, there was something quite familiar about the name. Now I can place it. His name has been in the news lately. I must say that I am honoured to be in the midst of a distinguished writer.'

'Thank you,' Bojor said politely.

'If the play is so good why don't you put it on stage and give the people an opportunity to watch you characters on stage and get your message?'

'Seriously I've considered that option. I sent feelers out to different organizations for sponsorship. As soon as I get one, I'll get cracking.'

'Is it so expensive that you have to look for sponsorship to put it on stage?'

'Not really.'

'About how much would you need?'

About one point five million.'

'One last question, any profit?'

'To put it bluntly, no. No profit. It's a problem we are currently experiencing in the country. Stage performances cannot pay their way through. They have to be subsidized.'

'Are you thinking of bankrolling the production?' I asked jokingly.

'It's possible. I just need to identify the business angle to it, and presto, I am in.'

'We must celebrate this,' I said. 'It's not everyday a long lost friend suddenly emerges to sponsor a drama production.'

'Don't be too excited yet,' cautioned Ovigwe. Though I could see that she was thrilled by it all.

'Now you've suggested it Brume, let's go out somewhere and knock off some bottles.'

With out much ado. We got ready and went out of the house. Meka led the way and stopped beside a gleaming Mercedes 300 V-Boot. He opened the driver's door and settled behind the wheel.

'How does he manage with his left foot,' she asked.

'You've seen nothing yet. There is nothing any able-bodied man can do that Meka can't do.'

As he engaged his gear, my mind went back to the early days.

> *Even a limp phallus, like the detached head*
> *Of a snake, can bite supple flesh*
> *When the waves return from their weary journeys*

I had gone to Boy's High School, Port Harcourt to do the A 'levels. The school was different from my secondary school both in terms of size, architectural design, discipline and camaraderie. The piano caught my fancy on the first day I arrived in the school. I remember it was a Sunday evening and all the students were dressed in white, trooping into the chapel. The organ gave a tune, and the students followed:

> *There is a green hill far away*
> *Without a city wall*
> *Where our dear Lord was crucified...*

I just knew that I would love the school.

After the service, the hostel master posted me to one of the houses and I settled down in my new environment. Later, during prep time, I saw a slim young man limping towards me from the other side of the block. He had a cane with which he supported himself. His ease of manner and confidence in speaking made him standout. We said 'Hi' to each other and settled down in the classroom. I could not read on that day. No concentration. After about an hour, I took a walk, and strode in the direction of our lawn tennis court. I had barely reached the court when I saw the young limping man come out to me.

'Boy, so you couldn't stand the heat in the classroom?'

'I couldn't, just couldn't,' I answered. 'How are you?'

'Fine. I'm Meka, people call in Meka.'

'Brume is my name.'

From then on it was smooth sailing. Because he was a day student, we spent only school hours together. He used to drive to school in his father's old Toyota Crown car, which gave him a high social standing among students. This never got to his head because he mixed freely, without prejudices. He had only two friends in the school, Patens and I.

During the early days, I thought he was too playful in class. He took nothing seriously, not even the teachers. Later I found out that it was his own way of coming to terms with the fact that he was suffering from the sickle cell disease and that he could die at anytime, possibly before age twenty-one.

And all of this shall pass away, even before the end.

A sickle cell anaemia victim with the mind of a genius! When Meka told me how his special status was discovered, tears came to my eyes. He kept a mischievous grin on his face and tried to change the topic. After many attempts, I was able to get the details out of him.

Meka was one of the eleven children, born by one woman to his father, Barrister Ogbon. He was a normal child until he got to Form Three in the secondary school, when he was always down with intense body pains and fever. During one of such crises, he was on admission for nearly three months receiving treatment for a malaria attack that refused to go. It was long before the period of routine Acquired Immune Deficiency Syndrome (AIDS) test. After a series of blood tests, however, he was confirmed a sickle cell anaemia patient. His father was stunned, sometimes brooding over the imminent loss of his most promising son. His mother burst into tears and called on her ancestors to remove this curse from her son.

'Where did you get this thing from?' she queried rhetorically. 'Why you?' became a refrain in the family, referring to his ill-luck of being the only child out of eleven to have the SS cell.

The pain on his left leg was excruciating. Suddenly, he noticed that the leg was shrinking. Alarmed, his parents invited a specialist doctor.

'It's typical of some sickle cell victims. We will do our best to minimize the effects on him.'

From then on, his life became a nightmare. He depended at all times on energy and blood-building tablets. He wrote the G.C.E Exams in Form Four from his hospital bed and cleared all his papers. However, he could not go to the university that year because he did not process an application. To while away time, his father sent him to Boy's High School.

'It hit me bad. At a point, I was so depressed that I stopped taking my drugs. I kept asking God, why God? Why me, God? Was it because I committed an offence, that I was singled out of eleven children to have the sickle cell trait? Why then did you bless me with so much intelligence? Everyone tells me that I am a genius, but how I could be a genius and live as a sick person?' He was in this state of mind when he met Rev. Shimaiker.

'Rev. Shimaiker altered my life. He gave me confidence and restored my faith in God. "My grace is sufficient unto thee" and "In your weakness, my strength is made manifest", became a familiar and consoling quotations.

Meka read up any book which he encountered on health and in particular, on sickle cell anaemia. From his readings, he discovered that, sickle cell was a peculiar disease of the Black race. It usually results from the union of two parents who had the AS blood group. In fact, intending couples were advised to check their blood group before allowing themselves to be plunged into marriage. 'Are my parents carriers?' he asked. Soon, he became a master of knowledge in the field of sickle cell anaemia.

'The most shattering information I got from the books was that except we had a special grace, one would die before one's 21st birthday. It was painful and for a while, I could not see myself getting to age thirty. That is, until the Reverend took to counselling me. He was always in the hospital with me anytime I had the crisis. This gave me a lot of faith.'

Meka forged ahead living in quiet pain, a pain which he had learnt to bear. His zest for live returned, having told himself that, if he was going to die before twenty-one he might as well enjoy his youth. This carefree attitude developed at that time.

'Once I reconciled myself with the fact that I might die prematurely, I ignored all things, and saw any situation as temporary.'

He learnt how to drive, to take long walks, to do exercises, and to cook for himself. He promised himself that he would marry a nurse. It was at this stage that he came to Boy's High School.

And they left him to die by the refuse bin

His fate was not linked with filth
Though he was born in it,
When the bomber grew up,
He knew that the path of the shining light
Awaits all fighting wayfarers

At the end of the first term, he came out tops. This became a tradition, until he gained admission into the Faculty of Law at the University. He wrote frequently, sometimes not waiting for my reply before writing again. The first letter which he wrote to me, had indeed increased my sense of feeling with him. He wrote:

Fajuyi Hall

Brume Boy,
    You must come here next session. I mean it. We've got a lot to of dunces here who can't shine your shoes when it comes to brilliance and intelligence.
    I feel so sad that you are not here with me. Don't tell me that you have another university in mind. I'll skin you. Boy! How are the other fellows? Nweke, Felix, Patens B?
    Year One is a plaything, though the lecturers keep telling us to be serious.
    I see nothing to be serious about, what with all the general courses that they stuff us with ...
    Write soon, will ya!

Reading his letters made me feel like an undergraduate. I felt flattered that a brilliant fellow like Meka could say that I was good, and that I ought to be in the university. It added to my preparation to enter the university.

I lost touch with Meka when the situation dictated my going to another university. In my final year, I received a crisp note from him saying that he had been rusticated for one year for alleged examination malpractice.

"The truth is that I neither cheated nor intended to cheat. I was just a victim of circumstances. I accept my fate. The truth will eventually be known."

He went on to write about what led to his predicament. Two days before a particularly difficult course, a classmate, a lady had approached him with some questions. He was surprised when on the examination day, all the questions, which the lady had brought to him for revision, appeared as First Semester exam questions. At first, he felt flustered and tricked, then confidence returned, and he managed to compose himself to finish the paper. After the exam, he confronted her.

'Omasan, what's your game?'

She feigned innocence.

'Game, what game?'

'Come off it. Why didn't tell me the questions were real?'

'Oh that, I knew if I did, you would not help me.'

'I see. Quite logical, isn't it? Selfishly logical.'

'Self first.'

'I can't argue with you. But tell me, how did you get those questions?'

'Top secret.'

'You stole them?'

'Stole? No such thing. Do you really expect me to tell you the source?'

'If you have come this far with me, why can't you just let me know how you got the exam questions?'

'Better stay out of it.'

' Do you know you can get into trouble?'

'Not a chance.'

'You seem so confident.'

'Sure. I have to be to get on.'

'You sure fooled me. But let me assure you that if anything blows, I'll talk.'

'And you expect to stay out of trouble?'

With that, she glided away, a beauty queen in her own right, using her only asset to better herself and soil others.

> *and so they tied him up and asked for an answer*
> *he asked for water to quench his thirst*
> *and they gave him poisoned liquid*

* * *

Three days later.

'Have you heard?'

'What?'

'LAW 310 leaked.'

'Really.'

'Oh yes.'

'How did it leak?'

'Only God knows.'

God and Omasan. And the lecturer, perhaps!

It was not only God who knew. Omasan's friend wrote a petition to the Dean of the Faculty, accusing her friend of stealing questions from the lecturer's house. She claimed to have written the letter in order to rid her conscience of guilt. The truth, as it was later discovered, was that Omasan did not tell her friend that the questions were real. She got to know the truth only after the exam.

Meka went to the faculty two weeks later. A notice was on the Board inviting him to testify before a probe panel on the Exam Question leakage. His nightmare had begun. They had been found guilty even before they appeared before the panel. He was rusticated for a session.

He managed to cope with the stress, staying at home while his mates went to school. In all of this, he found strength in his mother's faith in him, strongly contending that her son could not have cheated in an exam. At the end of the period, he went back to school.

*for some, it was just another crime
committed by another student
on the road to getting on in life*

* * *

Meka invited us to his office to finalize the production deal. During dinner, he requested that we avoid discussing the issue of the production. He simply wanted to enjoy the evening with his friends. The dinner went well. Discussions ranged from national politics to the role of women in national affairs. At a point, the issue of the General who insisted on accompanying his guest when the latter was arrested came up.

'That was honourable, a perfect gentleman, a man of his word. We have very few of such men left these days,' argued Bojor.

'Have you looked at the whole matter from another angle? Have you given a thought to the wife and children of the martyred General? Given the choice, would they have permitted their breadwinner to die for the sake of one man and leave them in the lurch?' Meka asked.

'He couldn't have done otherwise,' I said, 'it would have been against all moral consideration to hand over one's guest to fierce looking hooligans dressed in uniforms.'

'What has his death given to the country? It did not prevent the outbreak of war. It did not stop the pogrom. So what are you talking about?'

'I think all of this is getting too serious for a celebration dinner,' Ovigwe cut in. 'Why don't we simply leave and savour the taste of the meal as we glide off in that beautiful Mercedes Benz.'

'With all pleasure,' Meka said politely. Standing up, he signalled the waiter and cleared the bill. I spied on it and saw about four zeros added to five. One meal! Meka dropped us off after we had fixed the meeting for Tuesday of the next week.

Before the meeting, we had our own meeting and decided on preparing two budgets. The first budget was low keyed, reducing to barest minimum all costs, particularly fees for the Director and his Assistant. Of course, it was agreed as a man trained in the theatre, I should direct the play. The second budget was more ambitious because we made provisions for a very large cast, extras, publicity and a generous allowance for the Director and members of the technical crew. We decided that we would present the two budgets to him, taking time to explain the advantages and disadvantages of both.

While we were preparing for the meeting, an air of expectancy hung around us. It was as if an explosion was going to take place that would alter all our lives. At the time, I did not know what it was but I simply had a strong feeling that we had entered into a period of lost innocence and that all our previous calculations would be changed. It gave us great hope and optimism that we were going to have an opportunity to create something that would influence our social environment. Rastaman caught it during one of our rendezvous at Lagoon front.

Three horizons ascend the sky
Watering earth's palate
With promised meals
Of transformed visions
A stranger till yesterday
Bought the blazing daylight
And brought us little men
Into the armpits of figures

Brother, do not fade gently
Into the abyss of the future

We shall carry the world
And face the slaughter of the dangerous ones
We shall conquer them with them weapon
And create a new world for the children of Jah

This waiting brother can break the heart
And tear into pieces all the clothes which
Grandmama gave us.

He had written this poem in a moment of apartness, a moment in which he would move away from all of us and use a pencil to scribble something in his ever present pocket diary. We all read the poem. When it was Ovigwe's turn to read it, Rastaman broke into a song:

It was a little hope
Brother,
But the little hope turn big
They bring down Babylon
With their hope
With their hope
They bombed Babylon

Babylon came down
And hope took them away
Across Jah's wide seas
Into another Babylon
And Babylon said:
I am Great
I shall never fall

When it was time to return
Babylon locked them up in a tight fight.

We all enjoyed the tune but somehow Rastaman's song reminded me of Bojor's grandmother in the village.

* * *

The meeting with Meka turned out to be very fruitful. It lasted two and a half hours, though the real discussion was about an hour and a half. In the office, I saw a different Meka. His office was furnished with expensive looking furniture and carpet. His secretary was an example of efficiency. She ensured that all our discussions were recorded in short hand and produced before we ended the meeting. Everything was well ordered including our discussions. He was very business-like and detached from all sentiments. He took time to read the budget proposal and asked penetrating questions. He also discussed the play with us, having read it the week before. I was greatly delighted that he showed so much interest in the radical issues espoused in the play. With his bourgeois background, I had thought that he would be on the side of the oppressors. He even offered suggestions on how to make the production a huge success.

'Get artistes that are good and known to the public, that way you will give the play some publicity. The big names would attract crowds to the theatre.'

'They are expensive to get,' I said, 'because they consider themselves to be superstars in the theatre. Sometimes they get arrogant and become difficult to manage.'

'Well, all over the world successful artistes tend to have big egos. It is the duty of the Director to select a cast that he can work with.' Bojor said.

'Never mind,' Meka said. 'Just get them and I'll handle negotiations. We need a very big and successful show to attract attention. Nothing should be too much to achieve such a goal. I am sure we will all smile at the end.'

Most of the time, Bojor was silent and spoke only when it was absolutely necessary. He was no longer the chatty and expansive speaker that I had known. I didn't know if it was mere uncertainty or whether it was a mixed feeling over the staging of his first play. Whatever it was, the joy of the moment enraptured me and I did not have time to brood over a friend's silence.

Rehearsals for the production commenced two weeks after we signed the official agreement with Meka. The Arts Theatre of the university was the chosen venue because of its centrality and its relatively affordable cost. With a total cast of about thirty, it was indeed a trying time for me to manage the eccentricities of some of the artistes. Some of them came to rehearsals slightly drunk and perpetually broke. The weekly stipends, which we offered for transport, quickly went into beer and cigarette consumption. It became clear to me that some of the big artistes were only big in name and not in financial security. Occasionally, I took some of them to dinner and ensured that our evenings were happy ones. Before the end of the rehearsals, I made friends with quite a number of them. The most memorable person in the group was the Stage Manager. "Thatcher", as she was called went about her job with the strength of an ox and the commanding presence of a Grand Matron. Her jutting posterior, distended and huge, was the target of jokes, which she ignored. She managed the cast well and reduced my anxious moments.

Unknown to us, Meka had figured out the business angle to the production. He secured commitments from three of his corporate clients to buy theatre seats for three nights at very high rates. He also arranged for five other nights of production, open to the public. The clincher came from a private television's request to film and air the play after the stage production. Both Bojor and the Director of the play were contacted before the agreement was signed.

Six weeks later, the play opened at the Exclusive Auditorium of State Oil Incorporated. The auditorium with a 2,500 sitting-capacity was fully occupied by the audience. I went through great tension during the opening night. My mind exaggerated slight slips. When a cue was missed, I thought the production was going to be a bomb. Slowly the play picked it its tempo and the audience got carried away. Bojor watched the production from the back seat in the auditorium. He was clad in a native material designed like a free, big shirt. Under his seat was a small bottle of whisky, which he sipped from time to time.

Perhaps what increased the level of tension was the conflict between actors and producers of the play during the rehearsals. Every Director knows that actors and actresses act crazy sometimes. But once the frequency of madness becomes too high, one is compelled to worry. Sometimes such conflicts arise out of sheer jealousy on the part of the actress, who felt another actress was getting a better deal out of the show. At other times, they would fight the Stage Manager over welfare arrangements. Two nights to the production, the lead artist who played the role of the dictator in the play slipped into his blue period, a period in which nothing he did came through. At such times, liquor would be his companion. As the director, I acted fast. The double cast was given extra rehearsal time, different from the regular schedules. He picked up very fast, though he could not be as good Anobi Anonobi.

Anobi Anonobi was an actor of immense talents. He had played major roles in different productions. At his best he was a delight to any audience. He put life into dead scripts. As a result, he was invariably in all productions. He made money, though he was potentially broke because of his alcoholism. Yet everyone kept him as standby or kept a standby on him if he did any production. Once, he was said to have travelled out of town on the eve of a major production, in which he was starring. Later it was reported that he travelled to his village to see his mother, who had been sending frantic messages to him for the past six months. That he chose the eve of a production showed how reliable he could be.

For the production of Bojor's play, we were not sure whether he would show up. Till he got into his costume and electrified the stage with his colourful personality, no one was sure of anything.

The applause that followed the last scene brought me back to the present. There was only one person I wanted to see, Bojor. As I guessed, he was in hiding, inside the dressing room. We embraced each other. I could see the tears in his eyes. There were no words. Only emotions conveyed through silence.

Together we came back to the auditorium. Most guests were already on their way out. We mounted the stage together, joined the cast and took a bow. After this, order vanished and organized chaos took over. Journalists and friends besieged us and "Congratulations" rent the air.

Bojor burst into tears.

When we got home, the three of us, Ovigwe, Bojor, and I, it was twelve midnight. Bojor and Ovigwe teased me about my long awaited sweetheart who was due to visit anytime from London. I wished them well and hoped that the union of tonight would bring forth fruits meant for the future. Ovigwe gave me a warning look and disappeared like a comfortable cat into the comfort of Bojor's room.

I crashed into bed and dreamt of flying in the clouds followed by fast flying airplanes, which could never overtake me. In the flight, I distributed flakes to thousands of people on the ground, who jostled for them and waved me on. When I woke up, it was morning. The day of the second night had begun.

6

For five days in the auditorium of City University, we lived in a world of dreams, of dreams made real by the presence of actors and actresses. A channel road was built by this beautiful poetic drama between contemporary reality and the ancient past of the Akpo kingdom. Interlaced with cultural dances, time and space became joined by the language of poetry and the truth that is universal experience. The play, *I Shall Rise Again*, was a cathartic experience for me because it captured the essential ingredient of tyranny in any situation, and the reaction of the people. The point at which the audience screamed "No! No" to a character's awaited response to the dictator's question, brought to me the full weight of the meaning of the play. The character in question – Nule – is brought before King Orobosa and given the choice of life and death- life if he confesses to a crime he did not commit, and handing his beautiful wife to the Imperial Monarch; and death if he denied the offence. Although it was not said, it was clear that he would also lose his life in the first option.

When in unison the audience screamed "No", I was not sure whether they wanted Nule to lie and have his life, lose name and identity or damn the dictator and die. Later Bojor provided a third possible interpretation. They objected to the unfair conditions given by the king. Whatever it was, I was happy that the audience felt involved enough to cry out in condemnation of tyranny.

Two days before the production ended, Uncle Odiete arrived in town. I was too busy to spend time with him as I told him on the phone. He managed to come to the theatre on the last night to see the play. He was simply enthralled by the attention we got, both from friends and the media. The cast went into celebrations right away. From nowhere, music suddenly boomed and a cast party began. The Cultural Attache of a drama-loving Embassy spent time with Bojor and I and extended an invitation to us.

Behind the stage, there was a feeling of expectation. The cast knew they had done a great show and expected something to happen that would take the play to places.

Later that night, we assembled in a restaurant at Bariga, called "Mama Banga". Mama Eguono ran a modest restaurant that combined upper class mentality and a masses' approach in service. The surroundings were not so neat. Inside was a different world, both in the quality of the food and neatness. Meka had excused himself, after the show, saying that he had to get ready for the court next day. It was a return home for the four of us. "Banga" soup was a delicacy, which we usually enjoyed back at home in the delta. Here in the Federal Capital, we took time to savour it out side its home environment. Before we started to eat, Uncle prayed:

'We have come to eat here after a successful drama production. May we return here to celebrate something next year.'

'Amen.'

'May we go to a better place.'

'Amen.'

'May this play take us to places.'

'Amen.'

'Far away,'

'Amen.'

' …to distant places.'

'Amen'

'May we return after our stay'!

'Amen.'

'To our homes.'

'Amen!'

'To our people!'

'Amen!'

'A-a-men!'

We fell to and enjoyed ourselves.

'Bojor,' Uncle said, 'take over the world and conquer it. You have the skill. You have the talent. Don't let the people of the world sit on you. You may be small in size, but you are not small in mind. You are a minority man here at home. Out there on the world arena, if you excel, no one will remember whether or not you are a minority man in your home country. But after conquering the world, don't forget your home. Do not point at your homestead with your left hand no matter the amount of foreigners' food you eat. If you see friendship between cat and rat, you know that the world has changed.'

'I thank you very much,' Bojor said politely.

'But why do you keep referring to foreigners' food. Is there something happening that I do not know about? Ovigwe asked.

'No. There is nothing. But we see better when there is light. Your umbilical cord rests in the village. It must always call you, call all of us.'

'Amen,' we chorused.

The atmosphere became sober. When drinks started flowing, the mood changed again, and Bojor became expansive I gained more confidence in myself. That night, Uncle's parting words to me were pregnant: 'How often do we die before die?'

* * *

Some weeks later Bojor received a letter from the Lantana/Samba Association, inviting him to be part of a one- week cultural exchange programme between our country and theirs. Bojor was expected to give a lecture on a topic of his choice. This was the outcome of the meeting the Ambassador had invited us to after the production of *I Shall Rise Again.*

The meeting had been very informal. In fact, a writer from the Ambassador's country was visiting. That evening, he was expected to read his poems to a private gathering there in the lodge of the Ambassador. I did not ask why the reading session did not take place in a public hall. I simply guessed that everybody wanted to stay out of direct conflict with the Dictator. John Change, for that was our visitor's name, was a revolutionary poet who had seen some action. Our meeting therefore was part of the grand alliance, which the international community was putting together to raise public awareness about The Dictator's atrocities. Change told us about a programme for young and up-coming writers scheduled for sometime in the next month. We discussed the contents of the programme and all options were left open. After the buffet, we left for home and forgot the whole idea until now.

* * *

The Association was formed after independence by a group of radicals who found their way into business. Cut off and despised by their academic colleagues in the universities for abandoning progressive ideas, they created an umbrella of their own which gave them the opportunity and leverage to express their radical views in a comfortable atmosphere. Backed by wealth and political connections, they had become a potent force to be reckoned with in the affairs of the nation.

Among the speakers they had paraded in the past was a former Ambassador whose slave ancestry gave him a strong platform to speak on the poor-relation status of the African continent. Three former Vice Chancellors, safe from the Government sledge- hammer had also given widely publicized lectures under the aegis of the Association.

It was thus an elated Bojor who came to me with the letter of invitation. His black face looked flushed, and he wore a contemplative look.

"Boy, you deserve it. The sky is the limit. After what you did with I Shall Rise Again, just expect anything to happen".

'It's all happening in a rush. I hope I can cope.'

A great mind expressing fears at the time of triumph was not new. It was standard behaviour.

'Take it easy. You can cope. I know it and you know. Go get your act together. By the way any idea in mind?'

'Yes, for some time now I've been mentally exploring the idea of Repression, the Arts and National Development. This might be a good opportunity!'

'Good,' I responded. 'It will give you a good opportunity to knock some heads and punch some noses. Figuratively, I mean.'

I called Meka later in the day, in his office. Apparently, he was in the middle of a meeting. His secretary asked me to call back in thirty minutes. To kill time, I left the phone booth and took a walk down the street. It was the first Monday in the new month. On both sides of the road, there were traders perched delicately on stools with their wares displayed on tables. At different spots there were mounds of rubbish which had been deposited there since Saturday, the day which the Government in its attempt to clean up the country had tagged 'Purification Day'. However, because efforts remained largely uncoordinated, individuals piled rubbish at strategic spots on the thoroughfare, waiting in vain for the waste disposal vehicles to clear up the heaps. Sometimes such heaps remained there for three weeks, and ultimately ended up in the gutter again.

Near one of the heaps of dirt, a fat woman sat sloppily on a stool; dishing out Okro soup to workmen, who queued up, patiently waiting for their turn.

'Amala twenty naira.'

'Meat unko?'

'I say, Amala twenty-naira. Abi you deaf?'

'I no deaf.'

'Okay make you sell me wetin I ask you.'

'Yes sir.'

'Yes ma.'

To save some money, workers now ate food without fish or meat. I moved on. On the other side of the heap, I encountered a combined team of soldiers and policemen carrying out random checks.

Random checking. It involved stopping anybody on the road and meticulously searching his luggage and poking fingers into different parts of one's body. It did not matter whether the searched victim was male or female. Sometimes the searchers arrested some documents, which they considered dangerous to state security. Any material on the minority crisis was dangerous. Any book written by those considered to be in the opposition were also detained.

On this particular day, their victim was a sophisticated looking lady. She sat inside the taxi while the driver sweated it out with the security men. He had committed an unspecified offence and was asked to frog jump. When I arrived at the scene, a small crowd had already formed, watching as usual from a safe distance.

'Wetin the man do?' I asked no one in particular. A young man in front of me turned back, apparently to look at the face of the fool, who still thought that you had to commit an offence to be frog jumped by security men.

'You na stranger?' he asked, and walked away. I shut up after that. I was getting bored and preparing to go back to the phone booth, when the drama became more intense. The lady inside the vehicle came out and asked the soldiers what the offence of driver was. They ignored her, intensifying their disciplinary measure. Suddenly, the lady fell flat on her face. A kick from the rear ensured this.

She screamed. This seemed to stir the people into some kind of action. The crowd had since grown, swelled by the ubiquitous area boys. The fallen lady had evoked deep feelings. The crowd booed when the soldier flogged her and shouted:

'Fraudster! Fraudster!'

From a distance, the crowd started throwing stones at the soldiers who then got wilder. After a while, they carried their victim into their patrol car and sped off, firing shots into the air.

'If these men fit catch all the arm robbers in the country and beat them properly like this, we no go happy?' a man in the crowd said.

'Dat no possible,' another answered.

'Why?' asked the first man.

'Dem no go fit catch themselves.'

The other man looked puzzled. I figured the meaning of the last man's reply. 'We are in a real mess,' I muttered to myself.

* * *

A few days later, I read a newspaper report about a '419' lady and her accomplice, who were gunned down at a check point after she fired a shot at the police officer. The incident was said to have occurred at Ojuloro Junction, in the heart of the capital.

when I saw my mother, I walked past her
the police officer called me back, introduced
her to me.

'Boy, what's been happening to you?' I asked after managing to get Meka's office.

'I've been at a meeting. Where are you calling from?'

'Ojuloro Junction! Your meeting must have been a very long one…'

'You can say that again. What's cooking?'

'Bojor has been invited by the Lantana/Samba Association to give a lecture.'

'Good. Good for everyone.'

'He wants you to be there.'

'Sure thing! I'll be there.'

At this time I did not know I was inviting a member of the Association to the meeting.

'What's the topic?'

'It's yet to be decided.'

'Just encourage him to make it as thought-provoking as possible. The Association has the ears of the whole world.'

'I know. Thanks for everything.'

'You're welcome. I'm sitting on something big.'

'Really?'

'A million dollar pot!'

"Want to let me in at this time?'

'No. I'll fire you details when we meet later. The summary is that I've been approached by a group to act as solicitor and advocate to an oil producing community in the Delta.'

'Explosive, isn't it?'

'Yes. I'll tread carefully.'

' Please do!'
'See you on Sunday.'
Click-click. And the line went dead.

* * *

In far away Laguna, the man who led that country to independence was
forced to withdraw from the political race in what was going to be his
sixth term in office. After nearly thirty years, it was just as well. Fate has
a way with such pig-headed monsters. He collapsed right in front of the
media on the day he flagged off his campaign. After this, the local and
foreign media made mincemeat of him.

*Death appears to be the only democratic tool in the leadership
struggle on the Continent.*
Men get applauded for misdeeds.

Bojor's lecture must be deep enough to generate a lively debate in
the country. It's two weeks away isn't it? Power!

When power becomes too familiar to a stranger to power,
the people become strangers to him.
The meeting and departure points are worlds apart.

When we arrived at the imposing lecture hall, there were a few cars
in the parking lot. My heart fell when I saw the number of people in the
hall.
'Looks like the heavy advertisement did not make an impact.'
'Seems so,' Bojor said soberly.
From the side of the entrance, Meka dressed in a complete suit
swooped on us.
'Great fellas, you are welcome.' Seeing disappointment written in
the face of my friend, he said:
'Don't let the small audience fool you. Give another ten minutes
and there will be no space for you.'
'How are you so sure?'
'Just wait and see. Bojor, how is the whole thing coming up?'
'Fine.'
At such moments, Bojor never said much. Once I asked him why
and he replied:
'I've got to store my energy for the real stuff.'
'Exchanging views before the real thing just sharpens appetite.'
'It has a negative effect on me.'

101

'Take the front row,' Meka's voice brought me back to the present. After the introduction, Bojor will find his way to the high table.'

'You seem to be…'

'Just wait and see. Curiosity kills the cat.'

'Curiosity is also the hallmark of genius.'

'Hmm…'

We sat down after nodding greetings to some young men in the second row. On the other side of the aisle, a well-fed toad of a man squatted in a cushion chair, specially brought in for him. He looked like a man who had lived inside power all his life and had become so used to it that he ate and spat it, slept it and kicked it as he wished.

'Who's that fellow?' I asked Meka, indicating the fat man, 'the one smoking the pipe?.

'He is a politician and chairman of the day.'

'I see.'

Just as Meka predicted, in ten minutes, the place was jammed. It was as if everybody regulated his or her time to come in twenty minutes after the scheduled time. At twenty-five minutes past the hour, Meka picked up the microphone and introduced himself as the Master of Ceremonies. After inviting the guests to the high table, he spoke elaborately about Bojor, and I wondered how he got all the information about the Guest Speaker. Concluding, he said:

'Ladies and gentlemen, may I introduce Mr. Bojor Aruedon, writer and social critic, and a future Nobel Laureate, to you.'

There was a resounding applause. Bojor took his seat on the high table, bowing politely. Soon it was time for the lecture. He started by thanking the organizers for giving him the singular honour of giving the lecture. He questioned his credentials and hoped that he would not disappoint his audience. When he got into the lecture proper, his voice gained a cadence that I had never noticed. The title of the lecture was "Images and Phases of Repression.' He couched his introductory remarks in subtle imagery, drawing from the rich pool of African cultural history. From the second paragraph, he became theoretical. I have reproduced significant portions of the lecture below:

> Repression is the use of force to control the way of life of a group, a people, especially the inhabitants of a country. It is the devious art of forcefully and systematically silencing a person, an idea or a group for the singular purpose of ensuring the survival of a cabal, a dictator, an interest group, or an evil system. Repression operates on a convoluted logic, if logic it needs at all. At the bottom of it all is the belief that

the opponents' ideas are detrimental to State Security, the latter being defined by the parochial, selfish warped interest of an individual. At such times, State Security is determined by the viewpoint of the ruler.

The silence in the hall could push down a storey building. I looked at faces, including the fat face of the fat politician who came in to represent a corruptly fat government. The sweetness of Bojor's voice perhaps drowned the venom in the words, particularly under the circumstances in the country. Bojor's voice was still on:

Repression is usually synonymous with tyranny, benevolent or violent, and bares its ugly fangs or tentacles when acts of self-assertion offend the tenants of the power castle. It is not true that acts of self-assertion pose a threat to collective security, if the principles of governance are sound, fair, firm, and just. Usually when rulers become jittery over the people's reaction to their policies, they begin to live in shadows of fear.
Unfortunately for our generation, we are in that phase of repression when a dictator is living in fear of the people, he has been held in bondage by weird notions of security. He lives in morbid fear. The main topic in national discourse now is repression. It shows that the people really want to get out of it.

Bojor then went into history, including tyrannical strands and tendencies, which are replete in the African past. He spoke about traditional rulers, who sold able-bodied men and women into slavery for such trivia as mirrors and dry gin, and still boasted that they represent the people. "That phase," he said, "ended with the establishment of self-governance. If traditional rulers sell their people these days, they do it figuratively". He went on and on and returned to the theme of repression once again:

Repression manifests itself in different shades and faces, depending on prevailing socio-political conditions, the degree of insecurity of the rulers, of the power holders, the type of reactions from a threatened polity. A dynamic, vibrant polity would require a more vibrant and crude means of repression and subjugation. While some men and women are 'vaporized,' others get tortured and brutalized, and thrown into jail. In a docile community, repression may be subtle, indirect but potent still. More often than not, it is the carrot and stick approach: a smiling dictator chops off the head, finger, or genitals of a perceived foe, judicially, that is.

Repression attempts to control thinking, behaviour, action. It attempts to dictate what the public should read, what the public should not see, what the Press should write about, and how it should write it. The peak of the attack on press liberty was reached by the previous military regime, which declared that it was a crime to write on any subject matter that embarrassed any public official, true and false.

No leader, confident in his genuine authority, needs to suppress contrary opinions. Free speech and expression are the very ingredients of democracy. If the mother of durable democracy cannot stomach or tolerate dissent, what would her child do?

There was applause. He concluded:

When the spoken word at a classroom lecture or a rally begins to make the powerful machinery of state security jittery, then it is time we took a second look at ourselves.

In all human history, repression has never continued *ad infinitum*, no matter the sophisticated organization at the disposal of the state. Repression is a negation of the boundless possibilities of the human spirit, created by the Almighty to soar beyond mortal imagination. Repression is a temporary state and, as the proverb says, nothing remains hot forever, not even the heat of the sun.

Repression is evil, socially, politically and there is no human being who really believes that evil can reign forever. The post Second World War trials at Nuremberg show that evil has an end. Perpetrators of evil in any guise will eventually be called to account for their deeds and misdeeds long after they may have quit the seat of power.

Where I come from – an oil-bearing area – has been subjected to the greatest form of exploitation since after slavery. Although millions of dollars are produced from its soil daily, the people have nothing to show for it. If anything, there is environmental pollution for which the people receive no compensation. The story perhaps would have been different if oil had been found in any of the villages of the ethnic group that currently controls power. This is a form of repression too.

It is not too late to review the policy of repression, which has become a permanent guest in our polity. A guest is a guest. No more no less. When it is time, the guest must go or be asked to leave.

Thank you.

The ovation, which followed was deafening. Members of the high table stood up in honour of the little man who had spoken big things so forcefully and convincingly. Soon the audience joined and for five minutes, the applause went on until the MC took over. Soon it was question time. Bojor decided to answer questions as they came, not waiting to take all the questions at the end.

While some wanted to know more about the lecture, others went out of the confines of the lecture to drag in specific issues relating to the government of the day. His parables were clear. He avoided any direct reference to the ruling junta, contenting himself with the general effects of oppression.

'Mr. Lecturer sir, you seem to be afraid of the gaol?'

'Fear is the beginning of wisdom, isn't it?' There was general laughter. 'I don't have an Army behind me. So I've got to watch my rear. As a literary man, I am permitted to paint pictures, either artistically or philosophically.'

'What if you are dealing with opponents who cannot see beyond the given meaning? Won't it be just a waste of words?'

'Whatever that means, you must remember that dictatorships thrive on intelligence, sometimes, animal intelligence. The head of the junta may not be an intellectual. But he has the resources to employ the best brain in the land to think for him.'

'Intellectual fraud,' someone yelled.

'Whatever name you call them, they are never in short supply. There are men and of course of women, who are willing to put their intellect at the disposal of evil in order to satisfy their greed. It doesn't matter if they apologize later. A million apologies cannot undo the harm inflicted on humans physically or otherwise.'

A woman dressed in a tight-fitting jeans trousers and a flowing Adire shirt walked up to the rostrum, raised the microphone and said:

'Mine is not a question. It is an observation. Mr. Lecturer sir, thank you for the beautiful lecture. It was all so inspiring. I thank you. But given the experience we have had of radicals who later take up government appointments and sing a new refrain, why should we take you seriously?'

There was a booing sound from the audience. Bojor picked up the microphone.

'I suppose we are all democrats here, so let's give everyone a fair chance to air their opinion. Ms. Questioner, the dictionary has a word for people who make somersaults when their ideological commitment is put to the test. They are turncoats. But for their existence, such a word would not exist. Speaking seriously, as you listen to me, I would like you to concentrate on the principles of my argument. Are they sound? Are they valid? If you are satisfied that they are valid, you may ignore what I become when my spirit weakens. It is true that some of our progressive colleagues have had shed to their radical toga to take up lucrative jobs, but does it, for instance, mean that we should not continue to call for the institution of a government that listens? No it does not. The people may take a political somersault. They may die, but the principle lives forever.'

'A man should be ready to die for his views,' said a radical youth.

'Yes,' Bojor replied coolly, 'a man should be ready to die for his views. But is it not better to live for one's views? What have sacrificial, wasteful deaths brought us? In our polity, it is not wise to die on behalf of people. The death of a hero scares people, scares his followers rather than inspire them into greater struggles. So friends, be sure that after your death, your cause will die as well. Better stay alive.'

There was a prolonged applause. An official of the Association took over the microphone and thanked all the guests for their patience. He specially thanked Bojor for the brilliant and thought-provoking lecture. As the audience dispersed, a little note was slipped into our hands inviting us for a cocktail.

Even paradise has keys; it is not for all comers

The cock-tail was a fifty-sixty people affair. It took place in the reception lounge of the building, specially constructed to serve this purpose. Bojor got more verbal invitations to seminars, talk shows, and literature conferences. The lecture and its aftermath made one point. Bojor had arrived as a credible public speaker. At the cocktail, it became clear that Meka was the brain behind Bojor giving the lecture. In a way I think the discovery affected Bojor in the most unexpected manner: he felt that he was being propped up by friends, not for what he was, but for what friends thought he was. At such times, I was usually impatient with him: 'what does it matter? It's a question of

106

semantics, isn't? I never understood this aspect of Bojor's character. In this he was like a child. In spite of his brilliance and genius, he reacted naively to situations and he always wanted reassurance. The fact was that Meka organized the lecture. By chance I had asked an official of the club, how out of the millions of citizens and potential lecturers, Bojor had been selected, the official replied:

'It's Meka. You know his style. He digs into every angle of life. Somehow he discovered the hidden talent in Mr. Bojor Aruedon and recommended him to the Association.

'He made a perfect selection.'

'Just like him.'

What does it matter if the coconut was harvested
By the hands of a menstruating woman?

* * *

A week after the lecture, the Association of African Writers announced its annual prizes. Bojor's play won the first prize. It was the first and only day my friend got drunk. In his drunken state, he was fun to look at. Every little remark provoked laughter. In the privacy of his room, he got really plastered. That was long before friends, the Arts Circle came visiting. At a point, he burst into tears and started babbling incoherencies. He wept about the prize, laughed about the lines of mockery in the play. Pined over Ovigwe's absence in his moment of triumph. Suggested that he would need a poet-lover to knock out the night with. I wondered what the Press Boys, who made a national figure of Bojor after the repression lecture would say if they saw their hero crawling on the floor, moaning songs of sad joy, dressed only in his underpants.

If you catch me in my hour of darkness
Playing the master's song, do not think
That I have become the master's voice
Even I, I'm entitled to my little sins.

The press publicity that Bojor got after the lecture frightened him. A leading tabloid had titled the story "The Moral Force Against Repression". *Dateline*, a previously conservative paper, titled the story "Repression - A policy of fear" and added a rider "Writer calls for a Halt!"

Bojor was surprised when he saw his photographs in the papers.

'Is this how the media creates news out of nothing?'

'Boy, just enjoy the beauty of the moment. If the press has decided to create something out of you, then it means you have something to offer! For the next three days, Bojor seemed to have shrunk in size. His coping mechanism was a bottle of brandy. Between us, we knocked down three bottles of "Brigadier" in two days.

> *when you search for me, and my voice*
> *cannot be heard in the room, find me*
> *near the bottle, and this poem will*
> *be finished*

After this, Bojor's life became different. It was either one press talk or the other. He was tired and always complained of dizziness. He always asked me if he still made sense in his speeches or if he had started repeating himself.

'You are still on track.' I assured him. 'Once you derail, I shall pull at the ropes around your waist.'

But there was a withdrawal also, a removal from the scene, from closeness, from vivacity with me. There was an attempt to create a new person, a person whose steps were largely dictated by the flowing prose of journalists. It came in bouts and I had to watch carefully to be sure that I was not getting paranoid about successful people becoming bigheaded. But an indefinable halo hung around the hero, sometimes carried in a condescending look, or a sharp retort to a rather innocuous remark. For the sake of the revolution, personal weaknesses had to be overlooked. Later, I found out that some of those moments of withdrawal were spent with the flesh that provided a tonic to his revolution.

> *When the shades are gone, I shall see you*
> *As you are, naked, just like me, just like*
> *The others who did not make the journey*
> *But the tide urges you to make the book*
> *This shall be your testament*

7

Shortly after the 'Repression' lecture, different stars started falling into our lives from the firmament of things, which altered the course of our rivers, grey rivers, blue rivers, and rivers of blood. Some rivers were wiped out of existence, and some cannibals wanted to deny the fact of their existence, their history, and the monuments which their deeds created for those coming from the rear. It was a painful thing, this denial, for we expected those who should know to stand in defence of clean things. But they revelled in the filthy things that they did not understand. We did not really know the depth of the waters which we got into at the time, and how things that we took as hobbies could have profound effects on our lives. The stream continued to flow, yes, in multiple directions, and things were no longer how we defined them. Life came to have different compartments, and each of us had a long story to tell about incapacitation, about impotence and oppression. Some of the actors in the drama grew wings, with which they could fly for the rest of their lives; wings that we did not even know existed before.

The first and most dramatic of these drops from the firmament was the Fellowship Award, which Bojor got from the Guardian Foundation, to be resident in the host country for one year.

> even if the heavens fall to the ground
> i will call you my own in the presence
> of the enemy; with my head severed from
> my cold body, my mouth shall proclaim
> the bond of the blood that glues us together

We were in a boat, paddling across the lagoon, Bojor, Ovigwe and I. The water looked smooth like a stretch of sand in the desert. The boat kept gliding on though no one in particular was paddling it. Except for the occasional roaring noise of an engine boat speeding past, the lagoon was quiet. Suddenly, a big ocean liner appeared in the distance, coming at high speed. There were white sailors aboard, all waving excitedly, screaming loud incoherent words that suggested both panic and joy at the same time. Suddenly the ship changed to an aircraft and I was running on the tarmac, far away from it. Right behind me was Ovigwe. Bojor was alone in the boat. The roaring aircraft was chasing me, almost crushing me with its huge tires. Bojor burst out laughing. A deafening explosion made me stop. It affected me, but somehow it did not. It was as if I had been split into two. One part of me felt the pain, while the other looked on. It seemed that the explosion had blasted Bojor's boat. Granny appeared and drew a signal in space. Bojor was nowhere to be found. Ovigwe appeared before me laughing with all her teeth in a manner that irritated me. Suddenly, the ship appeared again, sailing on slowly, ever so slowly. The headless body of a black man was strung to a white dinghy, lolling lifelessly on the lagoon, following the ship into the belly of the Atlantic. I was about to scream for the boat to stop, and then a loud noise started hitting me persistently.

I woke up. Someone was pounding the door, calling my names "Brume! Brume!"

Feeling groggy and confused, I staggered to the door and opened it.

'Boy, are you sure you've been inside this room?'

'Yes.'

'Or have you been to the coven at Ireje?'

We both laughed at this standing joke. Travelling to the coven was said to make people absent-minded.

'I was having a bad dream.' I said.

'You are up. Get dressed. We are going to celebrate.'

'Boy, count on me. Care to tell me what we are celebrating?'

'A fellowship to Canada for one year.'

We knocked off bottles, chanted poems, sang and danced, in celebration of what was to come. Ovigwe was quiet through it all, occasionally forcing herself to join in the joy. There was a funny expression around the tight smile on her face.

Later that evening, Bojor cornered me.

'I have to pay a visit to Ovigwe's family.'

'You what?'

'A visit to Ovigwe's family.'

'I see.'

Ovigwe's behaviour now made sense to me.

* * *

It was the next day before Bojor told me the entire story. He started with Ovigwe's reactions to his trip.

'Ovigwe surprised me. As soon as I told her that I had got this Fellowship Award, to be away for a year, she asked, "what becomes of me?" I was surprised.

'What becomes of you how?'

'If you are going to be away for one year, what will my parents say about our relationship?

'I did not expect Ovigwe to have any apprehensions about my sincerity.'

'Then you underrate female sensibilities.'

'But, I'm not ready for a full commitment yet.'

'So what's the compromise?'

'We have agreed to make a formal introduction. You know that kind of thing.'

Oh sure. A kind of insurance.'

'Does it mean that she does not trust me?'

'No. Don't reason along that line. I think it's a precaution. You see we have had too many instances of Nigerians, who got to Europe and America and took a new wife. In a way, it puts her on firm ground. She would be able to ward off potential suitors, confident that her man is already committed to the relationship.'

'Sounds logical. Though we have seen cases of married couples breaking up because of another woman.'

'True, but Ovigwe knows that you are a gentleman. Once you give your word, you are not likely to go back on it.'

'But I've given it already, haven't I? I have assured her a million times over that my heart is not meant for any other girl.'

'But not your eyes!'

'As for that, who can stop the eyes of man from beholding that which is beautiful?'

'Just make sure they do not do you in.'

'This heart of mine can only accommodate one at a time. The rest is game, and Ovigwe does not have to know.'

'In a distant and cold place, the equation could be tipped.'

'"Love is not that which alters when it alteration finds."'

'Then prove it.'
'You are a good advocate? Aren't you?'

* * *

'When is he leaving?'
'In a month's time, Uncle.'
'In that case, I can't see him before I leave later today. I wish him luck. Just tell him I said he must always look behind him. A man who looks only in one direction never hears the friendly whispers from the rear.'
'I'll tell him. How I wish your language could be plain.'
'It's the language of prophecy.'
'What if the meaning is lost?'
'He should understand. He is a poet, isn't he?'
I had no reply to that. It was news to me that poets understood all things.
'And the matter of oil exploration and compensation to the people…'
'Yes Uncle…'
'Tell your friend to handle it well. Give it his best. Fight it with his life.'
'Uncle, how did you know about it?' I asked, wondering if I ever mentioned the case to him.
'It was in the papers, wasn't it? Besides, it is possible that the contact with him was made through me.'
'You mean …'
'I mean nothing. But at home, I was asked to recommend a lawyer. Meka came to my mind.'
'I see.'
Now I really felt like Bojor. Should I rejoice over the 'fat pot case' knowing that my uncle pushed the case over to my friend? Must life depend on connections to make things happen? Perhaps I was being too idealistic.
'You are young yet, there are still a lot of lessons to be learnt; in its teething stage, success has to be organized.'

That was what they did to Dr. Obomena, when he came last year. He was arrested for anti state activities, beaten senseless and he lost his hearing ability after the ordeal with state security.

He has vowed never to return home.

They think they can just freeze us like fish.
They may be able to freeze our movement.
But certainly, they cannot freeze our thoughts.

Bojor showed the letter to me. It read in part:

> The Canadian Art Foundation is honoured to invite you to participate in the Artiste-In-residence programme for the year 19...
> The duration of the Fellowship is one year. This can be extended if the Awardee so requests and the Coordinator so recommends.

One Stiffstrand Brickbottom signed it. Attached to the letter was a sheet, which contained detailed information about weather, clothes and other requirements.

'I may be away for a long time. But I will always look back.'

Look back! Look back! Here it was again. Granny said he must look back. Uncle said, 'Look back.' Lot's wife looked back. Pillar of salt! Look back! The subject himself is now talking about looking back.

'Uncle Odiete said you must always look behind you.'

'Uncle?'

'Yes.'

'When?'

'That's the last message he sent to you when I told him you would be leaving soon.'

'I see. Confidential, isn't it?'

'I suppose so.'

'You have a queer look on your face.'

'Really?'

'Have you become superstitious?'

'Over what?'

'Everything.'

Silence. Then:

'Is there a warning sign I'm supposed to see?'

Silence.

'Ummh?'

'I don't know. These coincidences are getting on my nerves.'

'You speak as if there had been other signs.'

'Perhaps.'

'Don't be superstitious. What's cooking?'

'I don't really know. Some coincidences are stringing themselves together in an unusual way that naturally, in spite of ideology, I'm getting jittery.'

'The hero at his moment of weakness.'

Silence.

'Beware of the man who is not superstitious.'

'Superstition is the child of ignorance.'

'And the cousin of caution.'

'I can see how far you've gone.'

'When you get to the village, ask Granny. She might be able to explain the mystery of looking back.'

'Is the conspiracy that broad?'

'You can bet.'

'She has been so persistent about the sojourner who never returned home.'

"The old woman will never give up.'

'On what?'

'On keeping me at home.'

* * *

Two weeks later, we set out for Dumurhie, Ovigwe's hamlet, in the interiors of the northern fringes of the Delta. Dumurhie was an ancient settlement, which was cut off from the major highway between Warri and Port Harcourt. Transport vehicles were available only once in a week, usually on market days. This perhaps accounted for the condition of the road that linked Dumurhie with the hamlet. With us on the journey were Bojor's young and vibrant uncle Salowo, Akpojotor, Otota the spokesman, a few friends and I. Because what we were going for was not the final and irreversible step, Bojor's father had stayed away.

* * *

Ovigwe, daughter of Justice Biokoro, grew up in the exclusive Reserved Area of Ikeja, in the nation's capital. As she told Bojor, she became conscious of her surroundings at the age of five, when her mother was at the receiving end of her father's kicks. She was shocked beyond words, and could only cry and cry. Nighttime was usually for crying, and of course nightmares. But this had not always been so.

114

Dafe was a pupil teacher at the local primary school in Ughelli. A dandy, he liked the girls just as the girls liked him. Apart from clothes, the rest of his money, he sent to his mother back in their hamlet. He lived on the village girls, all of who saw in him the potentials of a successful husband. By some miracle, no girl got pregnant by him.

He made no secrets about his many girlfriends. It so happened that different girls thought that they were Dafe's sweetheart until they found him out. In a year, he had built a reputation. Things continued in this manner, until he met Nyota, the woman with love implanted in her heart. Nyota came into Dafe's life and decided to run it, and he was too stunned to react.

Nyota never drove away any of her rivals. They simply slithered away, when they saw that a woman had taken over Dafe's life, running it as if she was his own mother. With time, Dafe came to respect Nyota, seeing in her, images of his own mother. Nyota sat him down and told him that England was her target. She painted beautiful pictures of London and how their lives would be transformed if he took his goal more seriously. He must give up teaching and read to become a lawyer. The way she said it gave the impression that London and the Law were waiting for Dafe.

Soon Dafe passed the London Matriculation examination and was ready to leave. To the surprise of no one, he went to "see" Nyota's people. Dafe left. Nyota was the proud bearer of the man's pregnancy. The arrangement was that she would join him six months later.

His letters from London expressed his desire for her to come over to the land of hope and glory. The truth was that Dafe had got used to her motherly ways of cooking, having his clothes washed, and bringing him money that he felt he could not do without her. She was indeed a surrogate mother.

When the baby was six months, Nyota travelled to London, leaving the baby in the care of Dafe's mother. She arrived in London one cold December morning. The cold was so bad that she almost ran back to the warm, slow weather of Ughelli. Dafe's passion for her changed all that. She responded. And Dafe started to bloom again.

Ovigwe came tumbling into the world of two loving parents one year after Nyota arrived in London. Meanwhile Dafe combined his studies with odd jobs, supported by the aid, which he got from the Local Council on the birth of his baby girl.

It was time to return home three years later, Dafe having completed his degree in law.

* * *

Back in Nigeria, Barrister Dafe Biokoro seemed went back to his brute personality. He suddenly saw how old and shrunken his wife was; forgetting that she had slaved for him while they were in London to get his degree. As a primary school teacher, she was no longer fit as wife to a Barrister, a high court Judge in the making. He started dating younger girls. It was at this stage that Ovigwe's eyes opened to the environment around her.

It started with her father's long absence from home, sometimes for weeks on end. He would return home late on Friday and sleep all Saturday morning. About mid-day, he would ask for food and ravenously consume whatever was prepared for him by Mama, as Ovigwe addressed her mother. He would then belch satisfactorily, rubbing his hand on his distended belly. Towards evening, he would dress up and leave the house, perhaps to return on Sunday night or early on Monday morning.

Initially, there were no quarrels, only cold detached exchanges of muffled pleasantries. At such times, he would go around the house, saying nothing to anyone, just no one would say anything to him. There would be coldness in the house that would ultimately be broken by Mama because she was not cut out for malice and small-mindedness. Soon, it became arguments in the bedroom, and finally violent quarrels in the open, with Mama serving as a punching bag.

As Ovigwe grew up, her hatred for her father also grew; she soon transferred the hatred to all men who tried to be affectionate to her. She spared some of her love for her elder brother, whom she considered a perfect gentleman, because he always took sides with his mother anytime his father became beastly.

When Ovigwe started school, she kept away from boys, branding all of them as bullies and terrors. She was highly individualistic making sure no boy came close to her. She went through secondary school, blissfully shutting herself from the heartaches of teenage lovers. In this state, she entered university. Not even her father's reconciliatory stance could change her. Shortly after she left secondary school, her father was appointed a high court judge. A month before the announcement was made Barrister Dafe changed his ways, much to the surprise of everyone. He stayed at home often and did some home things like watching television. For instance, he asked Ovigwe her favourite subjects, and generally tried to show interest in her private life. She just stared back at him, unable to respond to him in that aspect of her life.

He yelled something and her surprise led to instant confusion. The breakdown was unbridgeable.

After the appointment was announced, it became clear to everyone why he had suddenly become a decent father. It was a prerequisite to getting the job of a judge. The difference was only on the surface. Judge Biokoro became discreet in his affairs. Ovigwe drifted away, depending more and more on her mother to finance her education.

At the time Bojor met Ovigwe, she had undergone some changes on account of age and environment and was prepared to welcome any worthy man into her life. She was tough though, doing different things to ensure that any potential suitor was not coming to bully her. Bojor became one with her romantic illusions and strong ideological convictions. However, she still retained elements of her cynicism, partially accounting for her insistence on Bojor "pouring drinks" to her family.

* * *

Our party arrived in Dumurhie about midday, and we proceeded to Ovigwe's family compound. The family compound refers to where the patriarchs of a particular family live. Children, grandchildren to the fourth generation found a place to live in the compound. Also, women who had problems in their matrimonial homes were accommodated until the conflict was resolved or they got married to another man. Although some of the male descendants had built their own houses, important ceremonies and rituals were performed in the family compound with the eldest male in the family, presiding.

Pa Akpotive, the oldest man in the family, received us. After exchanging greetings, Pa Akpotive asked, who we were. Our spokesman rose to the occasion:

'We are friends of the family who want to become brothers.'

'We are brothers already, aren't we?' Pa Akpotive said, 'after all, we share the same ancestry.'

'True,' our spokesman said, 'but we make sure that we can feel free to visit you at anytime.'

'Oh, I assure you. You can visit us anytime.'

Just then the bottle of local gin and kola nuts were brought in. The kola nuts were inside a saucer. Pa Akpotive fished inside his breast pocket and brought out a Fifty Naira note.

'If you were not welcome, I wouldn't buy you drinks and offer you kola nuts.'

'I agree with you, our' Otota said, 'an in-law is never wrong.'

'Are you my in-law?'

'We want to become one.'

'I see. Then it's not a matter for my ears only.'

As if on cue, Ovigwe's parents came in. Another round of greetings followed. After our delegation had formally accepted the drinks and the kola nuts, several mundane issues came up for discussion. When the mood became appropriate, Otota stood up, cleared his throat and began:

'Elders, I greet you. *Okpako avwaren, your udova.*'

'The-man-who- is-crying.'

'The-man-who-is-crying.'

'Sees where he is going.'

He called out the praise-names of all the men, and concluded with 'Urhobo *wado.*'

'Eh,' we all chorused in reply.

'A frog does not embark on an afternoon run without a cause'

'We know,' Akpotive cut in, 'we know you have not come all the way from your waterside country just to say '*Migwo*' to us. Our elders say that a bird that dances on the road, has somebody playing music for it in the bush.' There was general laughter.

'The music that makes us dance lives in this house.'

'I was not aware that we have a musician in this house.'

'Oh yes! It's just like you not to see how bushy your beard has become except....'

'Are you sure that you have come to dance to our music?'

'I thought you said that you did not have a musician in the house'?

'You are not speaking like a man who desires something from us. Or do you want us to end this assembly'? As he said this, all the elders stood up as if they wanted to leave. Without prompting, all members of our delegation went on their knees to beg for forgiveness. There were more arguments until order was restored. As if nothing had happened, our spokesman resumed:

'The music that makes us dance lives in this house.'

'Ah! In this house?'

'Yes, the melody floated to us all the way in Lagos and suddenly we started dancing till we arrived here. You can see that young, handsome man (pointing at Bojor) specially dancing. It was he who first heard the music. When he called on us, we joined in the dance immediately.'

Pa Akpotive consulted with his people. While this was going on, Otota pulled up a bag that was squatting beside him and brought out a bottle of Schnapps and kola-nuts. From nowhere, a crate of soft drinks and a carton of beer emerged. All of these items were placed on the table with a saucer that contained a giant kola-nut 'wedged' with the sum of Five Thousand Naira. Our Otota coughed, cleared his throat and continued.

'Our in-laws-to-be, we greet you. Our son Bojor says I should greet you. On the table, there is a bottle of white man's drink. The sweet ones are also there. He has also added beer. In order to make the presentation solid, he has also wedged the kola-nut with the sum of Five Thousand Naira. Sia gware!'

'Eiyee'!

Somebody on our delegation handed over some money to our Otota.

'Our sister here, Ochuko, says that she supports the kola with One hundred Naira.' Support for the kola went on and on until finally, the tray was filled with money and handed over to Ovigwe's people. The gift items were also presented and accepted. After a period of desultory talks, the Otota of the host family stood up and asked why we had come. All of this sounded strange to me. I thought it would be a straight affair. Why could they not introduce the topic right away? Our Otota took time to describe the music that had brought us. Just then, the women of the house were asked to bring out the girl. A girl, the same age as Ovigwe was presented us. Otota asked her: 'Do you know these people?' 'No' she answered. 'She says she does not know you.' Our Otota stood up. 'This one sings well, but not as well as the one we want.'

This drama went on for a while before Ovigwe was finally presented. Immediately she came out, our women burst into a song. I wondered if so much trouble was taken to recognize or introduce a girl, what would the marriage ceremony itself be like.

'Do you know these people?' Ovigwe was asked.

Shy, she answered: 'Yes.'

'Eeeee….'

'Eiyee…'

She was led away and serious discussions began. Otota put it in clear terms that Bojor was going away for some time and that we had come to let our beautiful bride's parents know that we would like to keep her in our family. After mock arguments about how serious we were about our proposed wife, food and drinks were served. Ovigwe's hand had been secured.

When we left Dumurhie, it was about seven o'clock in the evening. Ovigwe joined us at the motor park, thanked us and quickly disappeared. By tradition, she was not to be seen with us. Was she so hungry for a man or marriage as to throw her self cheaply into her future in-laws hands?

Our trip back took us through another route called 'new town.' Here, we came face to face with gas flaring which the oil companies carried out. All around the area, the heat was intense, burning out all forms of vegetation.

They have burnt up my heritage.
Yet they want me to smile with them in conference.
May my ancestors visit them with the vengeance of the
dispossessed.

Bojor was pensive throughout the period we were in the Delta. At a point, I asked him the cause of his depression.

'Nothing in particular.'

'Better say it now and enjoy the trip. It's not everyday we get married.'

'Or you mean forced to get married?'

'You don't mean that, do you?'

'Every word of it! Why should human beings seek assurance by making other people uncomfortable?'

'You do need a re-training for women. What you have accomplished will have greater significance to you in years ahead.'

'Will there be years ahead?'

'What did you say?'

'Nothing consequential.'

I heard him alright. But I was afraid to accept the fact that Bojor said no to the future ahead. But in what way will there be no future? Remember to look back was what came to my mind. Try as I could, these thoughts refused to leave my mind. At Warri we parted ways. While I headed for Lagos, Bojor with the other members went back to the village. Bojor should go to the village and say goodbye to his folks. I had to be in Lagos in time to attend a meeting of an NGO on the environment.

Meetings. Meetings. When will they ever end?

We meet to discuss meetings. Sometimes, I do not know what my compatriots are really interested in. The environment or the dollars coming in from the struggle?

* * *

Back at the capital, I tried to re-enter the hustle and bustle of the city after the security of the village. Somehow, I was restless. I checked my diary to confirm my appointments. I found that the case of the oil spillage handled by Barrister Meka was fixed for the Friday of this week.

The next day, I attended a meeting on the effects of gas pollution on the environment. It was a good forum to exchange views on how politics was being used as a tool for oppressing the weak, and denying them of their natural rights.

The coordinator of the Environmental Study Group was a Deputy Editor in one of the leading newspapers in the country. A politically active fellow, he amazed me with the type, amount and quality of information, which he had ranging from microfiches to videocassettes and still photographs. On one occasion, I asked him how he came by such sensitive information. He said:

'At the risk of our lives! Sometimes we are chased by armed policemen who are prepared to waste us with their bullets.'

'Really? Your network must be really strong and reliable to get information on all oil spillages in the delta.'

'Our agents are all over the delta. These are innocent farmers, fishermen and women, boys and girls. All we do is educate them and let them know that what we are doing is in their interest. We initiate them into the struggle by showing them what silence and fear can cause. Sometimes, they come on foot to the town to reach us; sometimes, they send special couriers, human couriers through community efforts.'

'How come your response is so fast?' I asked this question because of a still photograph he presented which recorded the highest level of spillage in the country, up to 500 ft high. I wanted to know how his photographers acted so fast and recorded the spillage before the security agents took over.

'We are doing nothing exceptional,' he said, 'the fact is that the oil companies are very slow in responding. It takes days, sometimes weeks for them to react. Much of what you read in the papers is propaganda; it's all positioning. Often they allow the villagers to suffer for some time before sending the experts to assess damage control. The cleaners come later. It is supposed to serve as punishment on saboteurs whom they claim are always behind spillages.'

The meeting commenced at about 10.00am. The main issue of the day was the suit coming up in court on Friday. All strategies were weighed with someone playing the devil's advocate. When somebody raised the technical point about the location of the spillage, the coordinator replied that the village where the spillage occurred was in the same jurisdiction as the capital city. At the end of the meeting, it was concluded that we should all be in court to show solidarity with the community that had sued the government.

* * *

In the evening, I went to see Barrister Meka in his Chambers which was full as usual. It was as if I was being expected, because as soon as I entered the outer office, the secretary ushered me in.

'Boy, you must have had a ball. You look so relaxed.' Meka enthused.

'Don't let appearances deceive you. I'm burning inside.'

'Doesn't show on you.'

'Good cover up.' There were two other men in the office. Throughout our discussions, they kept quiet, watching me.

'Hello!' I said.

'Hello,' came a cold reply.

'Meet my guests from the Special Branch.'

'Really, pleased to meet you!'

They mumbled something.

'A friendly visit, I suppose.'

'Yes, a friendly visit accompanied with an irresistible offer.' The men stood up.

'We must go now.'

'Why the haste?'

'Once you make up your mind, let us know.'

'There's no need for that. I'm going ahead with my plans.'

The two men left.

'What's cooking?'

'You can't believe this.'

'I can believe anything in our country now.'

'Take a shot of brandy to prepare your stomach.'

'Not a bad idea.' He poured drinks. We both kept silent till we took the first swig.

'I'm all ears.'

'The oil case comes up Friday.' I kept silent and expressionless. I could guess what was coming.

'They want me to give up the case.'

'And they said so plainly?'

'Yes. They even added a pay off of two million naira once I agree to drop the suit, and a further two million, if I withdrew the case from court.'

'And you turned it down?'

'O yes! What else did…'

'You should have accepted tax payers money from them and continued with the case.'

'That would be fraudulent. I'm fighting against injustice. Why should I dip my hands into the mud of decadence?'

'Was there any threat?'

'You can bet it. That they couldn't guarantee what would happen to me.'

'Please. Have we gone so low?'

'I have it all on videotape. I'll make a copy tonight. You'll keep a copy. I'll keep one, and I'll send the original to my bank.'

Through it all, Meka kept a smile on his face, as if it was all one big joke. He told his secretary to hold on all calls while we went into the inner room. He pressed the play button on the machine, and the tape rolled. The chubby faces of two Representatives of Evil came on. True enough, they went ahead to propose to Meka in a very smooth way. Looking at their faces, they could have passed for two businessmen discussing issues with a third partner. But what issued from their mouths was odious.

'… We'll pay you the legal fees to the tune of four million: two now, two later.'

'I see.'

Suddenly, I didn't want to see it.

'Make a copy for me.'

Soon it was time for me to leave.

'I'll see you in court.'

'No come here on Friday morning. We'll leave here together for the court.'

'Fine.'

We shook hands.

'So long.'

'So long.'

As I came out of the inner office, the bell rang, and a client went in.

'Business as usual!' I admired Barrister Meka's guts.

Let the prophet speak. Let the mad man speak.
The man whose words come to pass is our true son,
our true prophet.

I got home late in the evening to meet a note hanging on my door.

For a moment, I thought that the men from Special Branch had been to my apartment. I guess I was jumpy. I opened the door carefully, switched on the light. The note was from Bojor. I scanned through it. Amongst other things, he wrote:

> My departure was not so warm as I expected it to be. Mama was all in tears, though I told her that my trip would last only a year. She said that she suspected that I would not return once I started enjoying life in the white man's land. It took all my will to extricate myself from the scene.
> Granny kept asking after you. What's on between you two? You must tell me.
> See you soon.

I was tired, dead tired. I crashed into bed and went out like a lamp. When I woke up, it was day. After a quick bath, I headed for Bojor's. He was up and about. Anyone looking at us would think that we had not seen each other for years. A four-day separation was long enough to bring out our emotions. I gave him a low down and we both set out for Meka's.

* * *

'I'm enjoying all of this,' Meka said, as we boarded the car. 'They are ready to pay off millions to a lawyer in an illegal manner, yet they are not willing to spend a kobo on the oppressed people.'

'I think they are only interested because judgement against the government would open the flood gate of litigations,' Bojor said.

'Be sure that they will also try to bribe the judge, if they fail with you.' I said.

'Judge Coleman is not likely to bend. In fact I was pleasantly surprised to hear that the matter had been assigned to the only judge who has the liver to say the truth, no matter whose ox is gored,' Meka said.

'Possible that Special Branch was asleep when the matter came up.'

'Well, in a few minutes time, we'll be there.'

There was a horde of journalists in the court premises.

'The Press seems to be aware of the matter,' I observed.

'Aware? That's an understatement. They already know the details. At such times, one needs close friends.'

I had a feeling that Meka had spread the word himself.

Does it really matter if the droppings land
on the head of the president?
Whose skull is better prepared to carry
the shit of foreign birds than the man
whose thievery fills their vaults with blood?

Judge Coleman came into the court at exactly 9.00am. A no-nonsense fellow, his reputation went before him, infusing dread and admiration in all those who encountered him in the court. Although he was the most Senior Judge in the Province, somehow, the headship of the judiciary managed to elude him anytime it became vacant. If he felt insulted, he never showed it. Nobody could read his emotions. He had neither friend nor foe. He handled all sensitive issues in the judiciary. What finally won him his reputation was the fact that he sentenced the son of a General to two years imprisonment for some offence. The heavens did not fall. He never socialized, and was said to have a penchant for reading novels, all types, far into the night. It was the only luxury he permitted himself.

Being the first day, the court was only able to note who was appearances. Defence counsel was absent.

'If by the next sitting, defence is not represented, I'll give my verdict.' It was such an anti-climax to me. I had had these hot feelings in my belly expecting to see a verbal war. But no such thing! The matter was adjourned.

'State counsel usually play such tricks. They use it to buy time,' Meka said as we drove out of the court premises.

'It means I shall be away when the case comes up for hearing,' Bojor said.

'Too bad,' Meka said. 'I would have loved you to be here.'

'I'll be here in spirit.'

At the intersection between Biola and Niran streets, Meka dropped us off. We waved him bye.

'Boy, we have got to talk.'

'I'm all yours.'

'Let's go somewhere…'

We went to Pat's Place, a middle class restaurant cum bar along Abiola Street. At Pat's you could have any form of privacy. Bojor's particular attention was Pat herself, a friend of his from childhood. They had been to University together after primary and secondary education. Her husband Dukefe had been doing well in a bank until the banking industry went burst. At the peak of his career, she had been able to wrest some money from him to set up the Restaurant business.

He had objected to her going back to work for someone else, and had put her on a monthly allowance which was enough to keep her going. But Pat was a restless person. As she put it to her husband:

'I want to work and earn money, my own money. I wanted to feel useful.'

She stopped herself from saying that what happens if suddenly he is no longer able to provide for the family. As it happened, six months after Pat started the business, Dukefe lost his job. Nobody was willing to employ him because of the stigma which followed a failed banker. Gradually he came to depend on Pat. These days, he would come to the restaurant about midday, do the school run at about 2.00pm, feed the children at home and return to Pat's place at about 5.00pm. He used to mutter: 'This lady's foresight has saved me.'

*What had Papa meant when he said that
the joys of today are the pains of tomorrow?*

When we arrived at Pat's place, some of the regulars were already there. Loyola, the beer guzzler was already there, drinking as usual a bottle of beer. He was a credit worthy drunk who took to the bottle to drown his sorrows. His wife who had gone to work in as a Nursing Officer in the London wrote him a letter seeking for a divorce. He went berserk, lamenting how he had slaved and starved to raise her transport fare, and how unfair she had become, marrying his best friend. He carried the now dog-eared letter in his pocket.

After we ordered drinks, Bojor said:

'My visit home has left me upset.'

'Why?'

'Granny.'

'Granny? How?'

'She seems to be saying something which I don't understand. She kept asking after you saying that we ought to have discussed the matter.'

'I can't remember anything special about her advice that we must always look back.'

'She told me the story of the cock that went visiting its in-laws and decided to stand on one foot throughout its stay.'

'Did you ask her why the story was necessary?'

'No. I just assumed that she thinks I'm just going to marry a white woman and remain there.'

'Perhaps.'

'But my visit to Ovigwe's family ought to have laid her fears to rest.'

'My advice is don't get hitched over there. Make sure you return home alone.'

'Trust me.'

'Sure?'

'Sure.'

The story of the cock continued to disturb my subconscious.

8

On the 7th of December, 19… Bojor flew into the bowels of the clouds in the air, wearing a tight smile on his black pale face as he waved us bye. His face wore the determination of a man who had made up his mind to conquer but who also knew that on the journey to the heights of success, one's candlelight could be abruptly extinguished. It would seem that he was not sure whether or not he would see us again. Perhaps I was reading that which was not into that which was. But the atmosphere was over-powering and there were no words from my lips; just a wary smile, a gesture to suggest the departure was well made. The cloud itself had no colour even though we tried to make things bright and happy. The plane that took him away was a never-return plane, the type that flew with anger, as if it would never return to the land where it took off. Its take-off noise was louder than the noise of all the other planes put together. The going was loud. Let the coming be equally loud, if not louder.

We were all there, Ovigwe, Meka, Ogbon, Gromyko, and I. It was a sweet departure, though Granny always appeared in all the photographs around saying nothing. Once I thought I saw her beside Bojor, trying to pull his arms. When I blinked and looked again, the image was gone. The paranoia had got the better part of me, I thought. Every one carried on with some joy that seemed to elude me.

> *The burden of knowledge is for the prophet*
> *Let non-initiates hold their peace*
> *Even the chameleon knows when not to*
> *Change its colour .*

A poetic party celebrated Bojor's departure. It was made great, interesting and beautiful by poetry recitation, story telling, dancing, jokes, beer guzzling, and pontification on philosophical treaties in a drunken manner. Through it all Ovigwe sat apart, not dancing in her usual manner. She seemed to be outside all of it, watching all of us with eyes that reminded me of Grandma's, and I pitied her for the far-away look in her eyes. The song that they sang did not give me any reason to dance. When I confronted her, she attributed it to the very idea of leave-taking. Departures, she said, always evoked mixed feelings. These lines:

> *I feel so lonely*
> *When you are with me*
> *And I'm so lonely*
> *When you are gone*

came into my mind. Yes, for all of us, Bojor's departure was a mixed bag. The seed must be buried for the plant to grow. Except the rains take flight, the dry season will stay out of doors. Who knows whether a prophecy is true or false until the appointed time? Life itself must continue, even if the dead must carry on with the dead. We then buried our sorrows in the cemetery of alcohol. He was an inspiration, a link to all of us, friends of different hues and with different tastes.

> *I do not have eyes at the back of my head;*
> *so I cannot see what happens behind me,*
> *who is going to lift the sword and cut off the life strands.*
> *Even though I have eyes that can see the stream that flows*
> *before me,*
> *I cannot fathom the depth of the river;*
> *I cannot see the riverbed.*

My parting words to him were a secret, a code known to only the two of us. Whereas Meka trusted me enough to give me the videotape of his encounter with the Secret Service, I thought that it would cause no harm to give the tape to Bojor, for safe keeping outside our uncertain and inclement society. I did not know at the time that it was a very sound decision.

'Take care of the tape, and don't forget to act when it becomes necessary to do so.'

He gave a loud laugh as if I had said something very funny. I was forced to laugh too. And he said:

'It's properly labelled. What harm can a traditional festival to do anybody?' referring to the print which he used to label the tape. Recently security officials formed the habit of poking their nose and fingers into anything that came their way.

By special arrangement, we went with him through security and saw him board the giant craft. As it taxied off, I thought I saw a black face struggling to get our attention from the porthole. He waved and the plane continued its run on the tarmac. Suddenly it was time to say goodbye. Ovigwe, Meka and I boarded his car while the others found their way owing to lack of space. The dispersal had begun, though we must return. Ovigwe did not utter a word till we dropped her off at the hostel.

'Thanks for everything,' she said.

'A pleasure,' Meka said pleasantly, lighting his tobacco pipe, a quaint habit which he had acquired. We drove off. There was a kind of ambience in my person, a languid, indefinable feeling, which I could not describe. From the blues, Meka said:

'I have received letters of threats.'

'Threats? Over what?'

'The oil case.'

'That bad?'

He was silent, slowly puffing away on his pipe. I looked at him. He wore a determined look, and I could see that he was not frightened at all.

'I have not told my wife. If I do she will hit the roof and woman me out of it all.'

'But you've got to tell her, you've got to tell someone.'

'That's where you come in. I'm telling now. In a manner of speaking, you are a witness.'

'When did you get the threat?'

'Two days after the Secret Service visited me.'

'Phew! Were they explicit?'

'I have everything recorded. Look in the pigeon-hole, and slot in the cassette.'

I did as he instructed. A voice, a female voice came on.

'Mr. Lawyer, do you want to leave a widow and a baby behind? Think Lawyer. It's better to allow yourself to be settled than to die young. Think Lawyer. I'll phone you again in a week's time. Make up your mind before then.' A pause. I pressed the stop button.

'It doesn't end here. Five days later, they called again. This time I was in my bedroom sleepy, with my wife and baby sleeping beside me. I pressed the play button again.

130

'Time is short.'

'Who is this?' the tape went silent.

'Press the stop button.' I did as he said.

'Naturally my wife was curious. For the first time in our marriage, I lied to her. 'Wrong number, I suppose, I told her.'

I paused for a long while, letting the information sink.

'So what do you want to do?'

'Nothing, I intend to press on. They are just bluffing. It does not stand to reason. If I am eliminated another lawyer will take up the case.'

'But you are different, you are you. You are a brilliant young lawyer known all over the country. Your appearance for the plaintiff can make a difference.'

'It's a risk but I'm prepared to take it. I'm not going to disappoint those innocent, oppressed men and women, who came all the way to brief me, just because some official hoodlums have threatened me. I have a just cause, and I am determined to see it through even if I lose my life in the process.'

'Please don't talk like that.'

'It's a possibility, isn't it?'

'What if we propose an out-of-court settlement?' I asked.

'To who?'

'To the callers.'

'Why?'

'That way the people get something, and you get something as well.'

'And we all live happily ever after.'

He chewed my suggestion over as we drove on. At this time, I noticed that we had entered the main road leading to Meka's house. He caught the look of surprise on my face.

'You'll be my guest tonight.'

'I'm at your mercy because I'm still wife-less.'

'Welcome then to my world.'

'A pleasure.'

By the time we reached his house, we had already agreed that once 'they' or 'she' called again, he would propose an out-of-court settlement that would give something significant to the litigants and take care of his legal fees. He followed this with an acerbic comment:

'If they are what I think they are, they will object.'

*Even the elephant knows when a foe
is digging the trenches of death around it.
The smell of death is the same even if the
despoiler sings a song of sweetness.*

131

When the hangman came that morning,
he said his prayers, asking forgiveness
before he executed the human rights activists.

We arrived at the entrance to the house shortly before 1.00am. Meka opened the gate with a special device, and we drove into the garage. Anne was in the sitting room, looking worried. As soon she saw me, she broke into a wide welcoming smile, expressing joy that I had come to their home to spend the night. She was a perfect hostess, Anne. Having a houseguest seemed to bring out the best in her. Meka used to tease her.

'The only reason I married her was her ability to receive guests.'

She would at such times, cast a warning look at him, replying:

'Each day there is no guest in the house, I regret why I married you.'

'Well you are stuck.'

'Don't be too sure.'

She went about getting the guest room ready for me, which was just a formality. Everywhere in the big house was spick and span.

When she finally left us to have our men-talk, it was about 2.00am. We stayed up till about 3.30am before Meka went to his room. During this time, we weighed all the options before us and made big decisions. After he left, I couldn't sleep immediately because my mind was still highly active. I ruminated over all what I had discussed with Meka, and came to the conclusion that Meka was placing a lot in my hands - if anything happened to him. I felt helpless and somewhat afraid that I may not have the courage and strength to do what would be expected of me if anything drastic happened. Who was I to bear the burden of a friend's problem? Meka, so popular, so well known was entrusting me with such a responsibility. Perhaps I had over-estimated the level of his connections. I had thought that he would have over a hundred highly placed people he could depend on in times like this. At a point, I cautioned myself against worrying over what appeared like a remote possibility. Telling myself that nothing would happen, I fell asleep.

When the snail embarks on climbing
The world's tallest tree, it does not
Fear a fall from great heights
It takes arrival at its destination
As a matter of course

132

When I woke up, the rays of the sun had filled the room. I looked at the time on the wall. It was 8.45am. As if on cue, there was a knock on the door.

'Come in,' I said.

A maid entered.

'Madam say make I check whether you don wake up.'

'Madam? Yes I don wake up. Where is your oga?'

'He don go work. He leave message for you.'

'Okay, tell madam that I'll be down in a few minutes.'

She left. Phew! Meka must have thought that I should not be disturbed and must have left for the office. I wondered how he was able to wake up so early after the long night, and leave for the office as if it was business as usual. I rolled off the bed and entered the bathroom. In ten minutes I was in the sitting room, where the sweet aroma of fried eggs hit my nostrils.

'Good morning, Mister Late Riser.'

'Hello, Anne! How are you?'

'Fine. Hope you slept well.'

'Sure. Where's Meka?'

'Gone to the chambers. Says I can drop you off there, when you are ready.'

'Well…'

'I'll get breakfast.'

Soon she set the table. I sat at one end while she sat at the other end of the table. We kept chatting on inconsequential matters till we came to the issue of keeping late nights.

'I think something is troubling my husband.'

I had to be careful. Fortunately, Meka had told me that he was not going to tell his wife about the threats. Trying to sound as casual as possible, I said:

'Why do you think so?'

'He's not been sleeping well. Last night, he had a nightmare, because I woke up to see him punching the air.'

'Why not ask him?'

'I did, but he volunteered nothing. Said he was in the middle of a difficult case, and that there was nothing to worry about.'

'Just believe him and rest your mind.'

'It's not easy. I suspect he is trying to protect me.'

'From what?'

'…from bad news! You know, from something that can upset me.'

'Is that his style?'

'No, but… you see, sometimes the phone rings, I pick it up, there is a cough at the other end of the line, and it goes dead. Not once, not twice. It's happened a number of times. At first I thought it was a wrong number. But when the same sound comes from the other end each time the call comes, I smell a rat.'

'Have you told him?'

'No.'

'Why?'

'You see, there's nothing specific. I don't want to appear ridiculous. He's likely to say that I'm adding wrong figures to arrive at a wrong conclusion.'

'I suggest that you discuss it with him. Probe him. Express your fears. If there is anything, he's bound to tell you.' I had to play safe. I did not confirm nor deny anything. The next question caught me off guard.

'Is there anything you know that he is hiding from me?'

'I wouldn't know.'

'Didn't he tell you anything?'

'We discuss a lot of things, I wouldn't know what he's told me that he hasn't told you.'

'Any threats to his life?'

I had to tell a straight lie.

'Not that I know of.'

Although I knew Anne wasn't fooled, there was nothing I could do. And there was nothing she could do either. But I made up my mind to warn my friend. Later in the car, on the way to Meka's office, she said:

'Please forget our discussion. I mean, I would appreciate it if you don't tell Meka.'

'Why?'

'No real reason, just that…'

'I'll use my discretion. I can give him the meat of our discussions without quoting you.'

And that was how it was.

Is there something like a reasonable lie?
Even if the pillars of the world come tumbling,
my love for you will stand like the hills of Ekete.
When I tell you that which is not completely true,
it is to protect the yam inside the barn.

* * *

134

Anne. A first class brain. Daughter of a wealthy conservative lawyer. Her maiden name had been too much of a double barrel. It was something like Akinto-Savage. At school, she was never spared from ridicule. 'A decent girl with a savage name,' someone once wrote in the school magazine. 'The Head-Girl of the school is of the savage family,' another budding mischievous columnist wrote. She ignored the verbal and written punches, attributing them to ignorance and ill breeding.

Meka met her at Law School and vowed that he had met his future wife. Her parents' refusal to approve the union was evenly matched by her principled stubbornness not to give up her beau. The conflict continued for a long while. Meka eventually won their hearts when he came out in First class at the end of the programme. For some strange reason, Anne made a Second Class Upper. Meka's brains broke the ethnic barrier, and he kept his independence by refusing to work in Anne's father's chambers. Instead he worked in the chambers of a radical Senior Lawyer. From there, he went on to establish his law firm. Although Anne complained about his stubbornness, she was secretly proud of his fierce independence.

* * *

'I think you should confide in Anne,' I told him.
'Really? Why?'
'I think she already suspects that you are into sometime hot.'
'I see. I know she's no fool, but did she speak specifically to you?'
'In a way, yes.'
'And what was your response?'
'My answer was non-committal. But I came away with the opinion that she should be told.'
'I'll give it a thought.'

* * *

I left the Chambers later in the afternoon for the library where I was putting my M.A. thesis together. I stopped over in my office (I had started work as a Field Officer for a foreign Foundation) to pick up any pending assignments. Certainly, there were subjects that needed urgent attention. I picked up everything and buried myself in the library till the pangs of hunger drove me home.

*Not even the bullets of tyranny can stop us
from shouting from the rooftop, calling the world*

to see how our own thunder has turned on us,
and we must fight the uniformed men
to wear the cross of liberty.

I left the library. While waiting for the first bus to arrive, my mind drifted to the events of yesterday. Everything looked like a movie. After three buses, I got to my one-room boy's quarter home. A note was attached to my door handle. I opened it. It was from Ovigwe. The contents were brief.

> Dear Bru,
> Just called to say hello and to tell you that Bojor called early this morning from London. Says he will call me on Friday evening.
> Would you like to speak to him?
>
> Signed,
>
> Ovigwe.

I was too tired to make any food. I bought a tin of milk, made myself a cup of hot beverage drink and wolfed down a loaf of bread. Before I ate it half way, I crashed into bed and woke up late in the night. My eyes were so bright, my mind clear that a poem came naturally from my pen:

> the snail
> bears its burden
> on a lonely journey
> its way is smooth
> from its saliva
>
> those who travel
> those who stay beside the hearth
> vomit saliva
> that ease the
> way for it

I read some passages from *Crime and Punishment*, concentrating on the writer's poignant line 'when reason fails, the devil helps.' Was the devil not at work in the country, helping the boys in khaki to eat meat from the juicy pots of the community? My mother used to say that help from the devil was no help at all. It's a trap. Aren't we in a sort of trap?

> *after giving him a plate of pepper soup*
> *they cut off his head*

Friday was still a few days away. I threw myself into my field of work, collating data on the number of teachers we had in the schools in each local government of the province. It was a telling discovery. In our lives, there are certain things we take for granted. For example, we take it for granted that there are enough teachers in schools in our environment. While visiting schools, I found that government schools were usually empty. The teachers complained that they never got their salaries. The pupils complained that their teachers never taught them during regular classes. Whoever wanted good education had to attend extra lessons, paid for by harassed parents. Most of the teachers did not know how to relate with me, thinking I was a spy for the government.

> *who knows the face of a foe*
> *when he comes smiling with weapons*
> *of love?*

A news item on the radio reminded me of the Friday hearing in Judge Coleman's court. On Thursday evening the announcer read a news item to the effect that a community in the Delta area of the oil province had been sacked by oil spillage, measuring 300 ft. To the fun-loving people of the capital, oil spillage was a news item. Nothing more. To the villagers, it was goodbye to aquatic and farming life.

> *I know the colour of your love*
> *It has the colour of black gold*
> *I know the beauty of my country*
> *It carries the succulence of wealth*
> *When the gold goes red, I know*
> *You will give me a red card*

On Friday morning, I set out for Meka's chambers, off Independence Road. Two buses got me there. The secretary, as usual, let me in. Meka was already in the office, though it was not yet 7.30.

'Couldn't have arrived at a better time,' he enthused sipping his coffee.

'Boy, you look all ready for battle,' I said, referring to the books on top of his table.

'Can't afford to be caught napping,' he replied, standing up and walking across to a computer. He punched a button and made a note on his legal pad.

'I'm getting ready for my colleagues from the Justice Ministry though I don't expect much from them. By the way, I made a proposal to my caller and it was spurned.'

'Outright?'

'They wanted to pay me off and leave my clients in limbo.'

'You don't mean that?' I asked.

'I told you. What they want to do is scare all lawyers off the oil cases against the government. Besides if there is an out-of court settlement, it will lead to a floodgate of litigations.'

'But the state is getting too vicious for my liking.'

'What do you expect from a dictatorship?'

'So we fight.'

'That's the spirit. Fortunately, Anne is solidly behind me. Thanks for your advice. She's got so involved that I am ashamed that I didn't involve her from the beginning. Sometimes, we are too protective over women.'

'All's well that ends well,' I said.

'A delegation from the village came here last night to report that they had received threats from our friends. They promised to teach the leaders a lesson.'

'It's getting serious, too serious for my liking.'

'Somebody's got to stand up to those bastards.'

'Sure. The die is cast.'

* * *

We got to court shortly before 9.00 a.m. The reporters were already stationed at the entrance of the court. They accosted my friend, firing questions from all corners.

'Are you certain of victory?' a lout asked.

'Don't you think that you are stepping on big toes?'

'From what angle do you intend to pursue your case?'

'Why not settle out of court?'

To all of these, my friend said: 'No comments.' It all looked like what I read in novels or saw in films.

We entered the court. The chiefs from the village were already seated resplendent in their colourful George wrappers. Meka went over

138

to them to exchange pleasantries. They stood up respectfully, looking a bit intimidated by the formal legal atmosphere of the setting. Government lawyers were not yet in court.

At nine on the dot, the loud pronouncement 'C-O-U-R-T' brought everybody to his or her feet. Judge Coleman entered, took a bow and sat down. The first two cases were called. One was between an Army Colonel and a woman on a charge of assault against the officer. The lawyers informed the Judge that the out-of-court settlement was still on, and asked for a long adjournment. They were given six months. The Judge warned that if after six months, an amicable settlement was not reached he would be forced to proceed with the case. The lawyers bowed obsequiously, and sauntered out, looking funny and miserable in their old fashioned suits and withered wigs.

He gave a ruling on the third case. Apparently, the victorious party came prepared for a celebration. After the verdict, it took the policemen nearly twenty minutes to still the storm. At this point, Anne entered the court, dressed as a lawyer. This was the first time I would see her in the lawyer's garb. It was an understatement to say that she looked beautiful. She was simply majestic and radiant. She got to where her husband was, gave a bow and sat down. Just then, Case No AS/1970 /666, between the Ologodo community and the State came up.

'I'm appearing for the plaintiff, your honour...' he went on to give his particulars. There was nobody in court for the Defendants. The Judge thundered:

'This court does not tolerate indiscipline. If the defendants fail to appear at the next sitting, I shall proceed to listen to the Plaintiff and award damages.'

Barrister Meka seized the opportunity and descended on State Counsel who never took the court process seriously. One of the responsibilities of counsel was to ensure that the court process was respected, he asserted. He spoke passionately about the plight of the people from the village, giving details about the distance which they had to travel each time the matter came up in court, carefully stressing the age of the plaintiffs and the need for counsel to be hardworking in the course of dispensing justice. Eventually, a new date was taken and cost awarded against the erring party. The next sitting was fixed for a month away.

Outside the court, the journalists had assembled again. They all jostled for a strategic position in order to ask questions.

'No comment,' from a tight-lipped Meka, did not stop them. To a particularly aggressive reporter who wanted to hear Meka's view on absentee Counsel, Meka replied:

'It is an extension of executive lawlessness which has been the hallmark of the government.'

The reporter wrote away. This particular remark came out in the papers the next day. Looking back now, I think destiny was at play here, because Barrister Meka had refrained from speaking to the press. The only statement which he agreed to make found its way to the front pages.

Anne joined us. After a brief discussion, centring on the overwhelming presence of the media, we parted ways. Anne and her husband left in her car, while Meka's driver was asked to drop me off at the office. We agreed to meet later in the evening to assess the situation.

> *if the world knows how the tongue manages to reach*
> *the tip of the nose, it would be more sympathetic*
> *with the complaints of the tongue.*

In the office, I started compiling my reports, which were due the next week. I got so engrossed with my work that I didn't know when the clock hit 5.00 p.m. I went to the restaurant behind the office, had a bowl of *amala* for a late lunch, and washed it down with a bottle of beer before heading for Ovigwe's hostel. Together we both went to the office of a friend of hers where Bojor's call was expected.

At 7.00 p.m. on the dot, the phone rang. Whose voice did I hear but a friend's from the cold horizon of faraway Canada! Our talk had no substance to the extent that he simply talked about his impressions of his host. I handed the phone to Ovigwe and the exchange went on for another thirty minutes. I moved away from the scene to give her some privacy.

> *do not let the cold weather turn your heart into stone*
> *as it did to the men who flogged my grandfather*
> *in the plantations*

Later, we set out together. Ovigwe was a bit talkative this evening. Perhaps she had been anxious whether Bojor would call or not. Even after the conversation, the excitement in her voice did not die. The Atlantic cannot break the cords of love.

> *your home shall be my home, and your name, my name.*
> *the voice of the river calls out to the swimmer only*
> *let strangers beware of strange ponds in strange homes.*

I got to Barrister Meka's chambers a little after 8.30 p.m. The whole place was quiet. Inside the office, my friend was all alone watching the CNN report on the federated Union of the Socialist Republic.

'Comrade Alikiyev is the sacrificial lamb for the break up,' he said to me.

'I'd rather sacrifice your brandy if you don't mind,' I said reaching for the bottle of Napoleon on the table. I can't remember the details of our discussion. One fact stuck to my mind: that his wife had hired two men to keep watch over him.

'Why?' I asked.

'O… she said something about ensuring that nothing happens to me.'

'Better believe it. It's real. At the moment one of the fellows on duty is watching the entrance.'

Here was I thinking that my friend was alone. Aloud I said.

'Helps the psyche to think that there is a trained bodyguard.'

nice people always get into trouble

We left the office shortly after nine. I sat in the front passenger seat while Meka drove. In the back seat, a very solid looking man, with a wrestler's chest sat quietly eyeing all movements. Our discussions were a bit stifled because of the presence of the brute in the car. I still was not comfortable with him sitting so close to us. I was relieved when Meka dropped me off at my place.

I tried to sleep, using all my relaxation techniques. But sleep was elusive. Somehow, my mind refused to switch off from the events of the day. I was restless. I picked up a novel, tried to read it, lost concentration and dropped it. I knelt down to pray, conveying my deepest fears to God. When I finished my prayers, I went into a fitful sleep. I dreamt that Meka, Bojor and I went to the beach. We were lazing around the white waters of the river. From a distance, I saw a boat coming in our direction. When it got to where we were, Bojor and Meka climbed unto it and started waving goodbye to me. I called out, but somebody from the rear clamped his hand over my mouth. I kept trying to shout and catch my breath. I was still struggling when I woke up. It was day.

* * *

I got to the junction leading to where I lived before I saw the headlines:

GOVERNMENT GUILTY OF EXECUTIVE LAWLESSNESS -
Lawyer

I bought a copy of the newspaper, folded it and boarded the bus that would take me to my office.

Inside the office, after the usual chitchat with colleagues, I settled down to read the paper. It gave a detailed account of what transpired in court the previous day, including some preliminary remarks made by the Judge. I read and re-read the news report. Being a Saturday, work closed at midday and I couldn't wait for the hour of twelve.

Filled with elation, I went about my work, burying myself in the world of statistics and figures and how these represented people. After a while, I got a message from the secretary that one Ovigwe wanted to see me. I gave clearance and Ovigwe walked in. In my excitement, I didn't see the unusualness in her coming to my office.

'Hey Ovigwe, it must be a beautiful day for you to be here…'

'I can see you haven't heard,' she sobbed and choked at the same time.

'Heard of what…?'

'Meka, Barrister Meka is critically injured, he is in hospital…'

'No! No! No! God! No! No! Don't let it be God! No! No! No! No! No! No! God! Don't let it happen! Please God! Please! Please! Please! Please, God!'

Everyone came out, and I didn't care what they thought of me.

'What happened?' Sobbing, she said that Barrister Meka was knocked down by a hit and run driver last night. She heard it on radio and decided to check with me.

'Is he alive?'

'Yes, in a coma.'

Please God! Don't let him die! Don't let him die!
Please God! God! God!
God! God! God! God! Please! Please! Please! God! Please!

Suddenly, I was out of the office, running to the road, leaving Ovigwe behind, racing to the scene to put life into Meka, to put the struggle back on course, to stop the bastards from taking life out of my friend, my brother. When I got to the bus stop, a car drove up beside me, and someone inside was frantically beckoning to me to enter the car. I looked closely and it was Ovigwe. The Foundation had obviously made its car available. Everything then turned into a blur.

'Where do we drive to?'

'To the house.'

'Where is the house?'

'Off Independence Road.'

We got to the house in no time with different thoughts whirling through my mind

Apart from the Security Guard, there was no one in the compound and there was an eerie silence that enveloped the entire place.

'Drive to Mission Crescent. No, first to the Chambers. Ovigwe please direct him.' As we drove through the streets of the city, life went on as usual with most people and there was no news about a radical lawyer being killed by an official murder squad. Yes, official murder squad. I did not have to wait to hear details before I concluded that the Security boys had carried out their dastardly plot.

The owl cried in the night and the baby died in the morning
Long live the witch!

At the office, I couldn't get concrete information. In frustration, I crumbled and wept like a baby. Before long, all the staff joined me. Yet Meka was not dead, had not died. Tears flowed! Tears of sorrow! Tears to show how vulnerable we were to the violence of the men who called themselves our leaders. I don't know how long I remained in that position. A man who bore a strong resemblance with Meka appeared from the inner office, looking calm and unruffled. With a quiet but firm voice he told the secretary:

'Please lock up the office, I mean the inner office. On no condition must anyone go in. Except his wife, of course.'

'And me. Yes me. Hello, are you Meka's brother?'

'Yes.'

'Please take me to where he is. You must.'

'May I know you?'

'I'm Brughoro, a friend.'

'Let's go please, he's been asking after you since.'

More tears flowed.

And more pains!

So they killed the woman whose son saw the moon
And told them that an afternoon moon called for
Caution not celebration

In the car, Dr. Nonye Chigalum gave an account of what happened as reported by the bodyguard.

Do not let the eyes see the nakedness of the ear.

* * *

After Meka dropped me off, he remembered that he had promised to pick up a few things from Lions Supermarket, which he would need in the morning. He drove into the premises of the supermarket along Wawi Street and parked his car facing the entrance. He came out of the car, opened the boot and brought out his briefcase from which he took money and gave to his bodyguard to buy the items. From nowhere, a car materialized, careened off the main road, knocked him down and sped off. People were too shocked to react immediately. The bodyguard sprang into action. Through it all, Meka kept muttering: "They've got me; they have finally got me.' Tell Brughoro that our friends from the Secret Service managed to get me.' He lifted his master into the car and sped off to the University Teaching Hospital where he was taken to the Intensive Care Unit, (ICU).

We arrived at the hospital after what appeared to be a two-hour journey. As soon as we disembarked, Anne appeared from the balcony of the building facing us. Seeing her dry-eyed, sobered me a little. Perhaps it was not so bad. When I got to her, she came into my arms, and the tears came:

'Anne, I'm so sorry.'

'He'll pull through, he'll pull through.'

Tears flowed freely.

'I must see him, Anne, I must.'

Like the miracle worker, I hoped that my contact with him would revive him.

'We can go in together. Visitors are not allowed to remain long.'

While we poured out emotions, Ovigwe and Nonye stood back, wearing long faces and perhaps feeling really sorry for me. I did not know that the attack on Meka would rattle me this way.

At the entrance to the ICU, we were asked to put on gloves, an apron, a mask and sprayed with disinfectant. I simply went through the motions. Face to face with my friend, I lost all hope. The colour of his skin had changed to a dark grey. Occasionally, he would mutter some incoherent things, and slip into unconsciousness again. His two legs were suspended from the top of the bed and all kinds of pipes went in and out of his mouth and abdomen. Gradually my grief gave way to anger. Faintly I heard Anne say:

'See what they've done to your brother.'

Yes he was my brother, a friend, a friend who trusted me enough to tell me the things he did not want to tell his wife. My antennae picked up the nuances of 'they' in Anne's statement.

'Somebody must pay for this.' I felt better immediately I said these words. Revenge!

'Anne,' I said as I piloted her out of the ward, 'I'll fight this with my last blood.' And I meant it, though I did not know how I would do it.

'Don't do anything rash.'

'I am going back to the house, your house. Nonye will come with me. In the evening we'll come back here.' I discarded all the paraphernalia with which I was adorned, and signalled Nonye to come with me. As we strolled off, an idea occurred to me.

'Nurse, please where is the Consultant in charge of my brother's case?'

I suspected she was going to slip into technicalities, and she did.

'Nobody is allowed to see…'

'Nurse, I represent The Guardian Foundation. Let's make sure we handle all things right.' The expression on her face changed.

'Come with me please.' Suddenly she became an efficient worker, leading us to face judgement.

'Please wait outside while I see him.'

'That's okay.' A knock and she went in.

I gave her two minutes. I was going to burst in when the door swung open and a pleasant-looking, chubby fellow stretched out his hand for a handshake.

'I am Dr. Debayo,' he said

'I'm Brughoro. This is Dr. Nonye…'

'Come right in,' as we entered the office, the nurse wriggled out.

'Sit down gentlemen.'

'Thanks,' I said, as we sat down.

'What may I do for you?'

'Barrister Meka is our brother. Please give it to us straight. Does he stand a chance?'

'Between when he was brought in and this time, he has shown clinical improvements…'

'Please be frank, man to man, understand? From your assessment, what are his chances of getting out of this alive?'

'We're doing our best, and we must leave the rest to God.' I stared straight into his eyes and he shifted uncomfortably in his seat. 'Sometimes, some terribly bad cases take a dramatic turn, defying all known laws. The cranium is cracked, so are five of his ribs. The two legs are completely fractured, hence the POP. There have been two surgical interventions in the last sixteen hours to drain fluid from…'

'In other words, his case is very, very bad,' Nonye cut in.

'You can put it that way.'

'Thanks for your frankness. I hope we can meet again under better circumstances.'

Outside the office, Ovigwe was waiting. There were no words, only gestures.

'Let's go.' I said 'Nonye, we must get to the office for a brief discussion. There is a lot you must know about.'

'I'm curious.'

'By the way, where is the bodyguard?'

'He's all huddled up in a room on the other side.'

'Please send for him.'

When Asoro (I soon learnt was his name) came, his macho was all gone. His shoulder had sagged and he could not look me in the eyes.

Inside the car I asked him:

'Where is your master?'

All I could get from him was a heart-rending cry that told me that the man was broken. Was this the man we entrusted the security of our friend to? On the way we dropped Ovigwe off.

* * *

'Tell us exactly how it happened, where it happened and everything that you saw,' positioning myself on the settee in Meka's office. 'You must be familiar with the story now having told it to the police.'

He managed to pull himself together.

'After we dropped you off, we drove on to Macauley Way. At the junction near Jobi, I noticed a car following us. I told Master. He went through different streets, round and round. They kept following us. We confirmed that they were following us. Then, at a point, we lost them. We thought that we would not see them again. So… so at Bode Avenue, Master stopped to buy something. He said he had promised madam that he would buy her something from the shop. He drove the car into the compound, came out of the car and gave me the money. Suddenly a car emerged from the dark, with no headlamp and knocked him down.'

'Just like that?'

'Yes.'

'Why did he stop?'

'I don't know. I told him to drive straight home but he said no, that he wanted to see what the men would do and that if they wanted to kill him, it would be better for it to take place in town than in the presence of his family.'

'Did you catch a glimpse of the men?' For a long time there was no reply, only anguish.

'Asoro, did you catch a glimpse of the men?'

'Oga, I will answer you, but make you protect me.'

'Protect you? From who?'

'From them.'

'Them?'

'Yes, the men I worked with before for State.'

'Describe them.'

He gave a description of the men and somehow the description matched those of our visitors from Secret Service'

'Wait.' I got the key and went into Meka's inner office, fished out the cassette and slotted it into the video machine. The picture came on.

'Do you know...?'

'Na the men. That na Alakuru. The other one na Andrew.'

'You sure?'

'Na them na him finish oga.'

We exchanged glances, Nonye and I. I didn't need to tell him a long story, judging by what Asoro had said. But I still told him about the death threats of the last two weeks.

'Don't breathe a word of what you have just told us to anyone.'

even the lame can be forced to defend his own
when his pride is kicked in the face.

* * *

The next day, Asoro left for Bojor's village, with firm instructions to stay with Granny. He meekly obeyed. I knew Granny would cater for him in her own way. He refused to go home for the night, saying that there was no need. No one would miss him.

The funeral took place two weeks after he was knocked down, and one week after he died. He died. Yes he died. We were at his bedside, Anne and I. The last thing he said was 'Remember the tape.' A bright smile lit up his face and he stared at us as if for the last time. He then stretched out, with all the pipes and gadgets losing their place and Anne calling out 'Doctor, Doctor.' The doctor came in quite alright but merely to supervise the process of dying. He was gone. Anne stood riveted to one spot, staring intently at him as if her stare would bring him back. The hospital staff started to draw the curtains and cover him up. Gently, very gently, I led my friend's wife away. In the car, she asked:

'Is he really gone? Is Meka really gone?'

*as for the baboons in power nothing can change
the firmament of their sky*

I had no answer. There was no answer. There were no tears. She refused to be sedated, insisting that she would supervise the funeral arrangements. She chose the clothes, sat in conference with Meka's family over burial plans. There were arguments initially that he must be taken to the village; others argued that he should be buried in the town where he lived and died. The matter was settled when Meka's father sent a message that the body should be buried in the city, citing tradition as one of his reasons. As a young man, he should simply be buried without fanfare. A father should not bury his son; it should be the other way round. For this reason, he did not want to see the body. The burial should be a solemn ceremony.

For the first time in my life, I got involved in the morbid task of burying the dead. The undertakers made it easier, though we had to be present at the Morgue, Local council, Police Station. The Police.

are you a part of the solution or father of the problem?

The decision to hide Asoro was taken by Nonye and I, shortly after we spoke with Bojor on the phone. Even before Meka died, we had decided that we were going to use our lean resources to fight the men of the Secret Service. Our trump card was Asoro who had to be hidden in a safe place. The first place that came to mind was the Priest's. We went to see him in the quiet lodge of the Church, far away in the outskirts of the city. He wore a sympathetic look and made the right expressions of shock. I thought we had won a convert. His terse reply jolted us:

'I don't want any trouble with government. I am sorry. I have to turn you back. May the Good Lord in His Infinite Grace protect you. Amen!'

and a man's foes shall be they of his own household

We thanked him for even listening to us. How would the Lord protect us if all human beings turned us away in time of distress? Granny, an old woman eventually accepted him, asking no questions.

Bojor's friendship was enough to guarantee him accommodation and a place in the family.

* * *

After the burial, the newspapers would not let up about Meka's death. From *Daily Voice*, where the editor was a friend in the struggle, articles came out regularly, stridently condemning the ineptitude of the police. Suddenly things began to take a fast turn. *Daily Voice* came out with an editorial, praising two officials who had been particularly helpful in investigations. The two officers were mentioned by name.

The next morning, a confident Commissioner of Police featured on an early morning programme "The Police and You." Our two friends from the Secret Service spoke smoothly about how they arrived at the scene of the incident ten minutes after the hit and run away driver had knocked down an innocent man. They promised to get the perpetrators of the crime within the shortest possible time. 'We shall leave no stone unturned in our determination to fish out the perpetrators of this horrible and atrocious crime.' It was a phone in programme and the response was spectacular because people called in to commend the fast-moving cops. Some rich fellow even promised the police a reward if they could arrest the criminals.

news is what they tell us

The next night, Bojor's face came alive on the television screen where I had gone to visit Shata. It was a cable programme with all the force of international presence. Although it was not news to me, Bojor's proclamation:

'We have strong evidence against the State that Barrister Meka's death was State organised,' made us feel better and it hit me with great force.

i may appear feeble to the world
but let no one call my walking stick
the brother of water snake

The interviewer probed for more information, asking the same question in different ways. The only additional information Bojor gave was that he had a tape of the men who had threatened Meka the week before he died. Because the men could not buy Meka off the oil case, he said, they had to silence him. I knew that the die was cast.

Man's survival instinct rises in the times of extreme danger, particularly when one of a group had been brazenly slaughtered by the men and women who had swore to defend the people and the land. Shata and I reviewed the situation and agreed that I should lie low. So far, I had not made any obvious moves. But if the Secret Service had any intelligence left, they would come for me. It was Shata who pointed out the danger of Asoro hiding in the village. He reasoned that our hunters would naturally go to Bojor's home and harass his parents. What if they found Asoro there?

Bells started ringing in my head and I knew that Asoro had to move from Granny's room. The move was not so smart after all. Shata locked me in his one-bedroom apartment and set out to look for Ovigwe. When Ovigwe was asked to travel to the village to alert Asoro, she balked, claiming that her studies were more important.

'Are your studies more important than the life of your future father-in-law?'

That seemed to shake her. The next morning she set out for the coastal region.

* * *

Shata narrated this encounter with Ovigwe to me in my hideout, and concluded it with a report on his visit to my office.

'Man, you are a wanted man.'

'You are kidding.'

'No kidding! They've been to your house, they've been to your office. All your papers are shreds now.'

'What happened in my office?'

'Of course they could not do or get much. The Resident simply told them that you had not reported for work.'

'Trust my boss to be tight-lipped.'

I remember giving him a few hints about my activities with the radical movement once. All he said was that I should be prepared for a quick exit if things went sour, and that I could count on his support. He went on to describe how uniformed men had stormed my apartment the day before and ransacked my wardrobe, looking for seditious material.

Two nights later, there was a knock on Shata's door. A female voice identified herself. It was obvious that Shata and I were nervous. As soon as the knock sounded, we froze. Ovigwe then identified herself. Shata opened the door cautiously, and she stepped in looking like a lost ghost.

'Ovigwe, what happened?'

She burst into tears, shaking terribly like someone in a nightmare.

'They got there before me. They beat up Granny, dragged Asoro on the ground to the boat. He was beaten to a coma in the presence of everyone.'

Silence. Only thoughts flowed. Outside, the night plodded on. Little sounds came to mean something to us. Any approaching vehicle made my heart leap. I had to do something, plan my safety and do something defiant.

'What are going to do now?' Ovigwe wailed.

'We lie low, and stay apart as much as possible. Ovigwe you stay away from here. I'm sure you are safe in your hostel. I'll be coming to see you there as the need arises.'

She stayed the night and left the next morning.

For the next three days, our existence went into a routine. Shata left the house very early in the morning for his place his work. Throughout the day, I stayed indoors, reading all available books, magazines and newspapers. I was able to read all the little stories which never made the headlines, which nevertheless gave me an insight into the apparently insignificant issues of the day. I read up all letters to the editor, concluding that some of the real truths about the rot in the country were contained in those letters. Radio stations, local and foreign became my best companions. I also took time to study the news slant of the BBC, noting the attention and prestige attached to reporting disasters. Often, before the end of day, I would be able to cast the news with presenter having been so bombarded with the same information over and over. Shata would return in the afternoon, prepare lunch and give me valuable information.

'Your Editor friend has been picked up.'

The net was closing in.

'Any charges against him?'

'None. There is a special decree, protecting the State.'

'I'm not surprised.'

Later that evening, as we sat in front of the television, a thought occurred to me.

'What if I moved to the campus?'

'Why? Aren't you comfortable here?'

'Comfort has nothing to with it. My sixth sense says I should move.'

'Tomorrow morning then.'

'No tonight.'

Just then Bojor's face floated into the room. We became glued to the TV set as we watched the station which had boldly produced footage from a CNN report. Apparently, the programme had been on for while, because the interviewer said:

'Now let's watch a clip from that interview.'

The faces of our friends from the Secret Service came on the screen. It was the tape.

'Those bastards will get mad now. I've to get going.'

In twenty minutes, we were on our way to the bus stop. Shata came with me to the gate of the campus and went back home. In the hostel, I stayed with a friend's younger brother, lost in the face of a thousand faces, some innocent and some not so innocent. The environment gave me a good opportunity to dissolve into nothingness while the hunt lasted.

The next morning, the papers had a field day, challenging the state to make a defence of herself before the people. Inside the campus, students were restive. The full weight of that footage came to bear on the nation's psyche when a respected daily dedicated its front page to the Meka saga. It put two and two together, matching the faces that appeared on the cable programme with those fellows who had sworn to get the perpetrators of the crime. Concluding the reporter said:

'Obviously the government has to investigate itself and bring these two officers to book.'

To say the least, the government was thoroughly embarrassed. It kept a studious silence on the issue. Not even the evil, loquacious Information Minister could craft a response immediately. Later, I read in the papers that Meka's wife had instituted a 150 million naira lawsuit against the government for murdering her husband. I could not phone her because I guessed her line would be bugged.

I was in the dark, not having heard from either Shata or Ovigwe. Although, I had decided to stay away from Ovigwe initially, my curiosity got the better of me and I ventured into the night.. I located her in the hostel cafeteria.

'Hey! Bru! What brings you here? Let's go somewhere.'

I got the message. We came out and strolled as slowly as possible to the classroom area. There, she gave me fill-ups that chilled me.

'Shata was picked up two nights ago, shortly after he returned home. His neighbours said that he saw his friend off and came back into the waiting arms of the security agents.'

'You mean he was arrested on…'

'That same night. You were lucky. Did you get advance information?'

'Advance information? Good heavens, no. Why?'

'It was so coincidental.'

'Yes.'

'So, where have you been staying?'

'Different places.'

Even as I said this, I made up my mind that I was going to move from one place to the other. If Shata was tortured, he could give away my hideout. I managed to smile.

'Here you been following Bojor's style?'

'Yes of course. I still speak to him.'

'Better be careful.'

'Oh yes we are. We use codes.'

'That's better.'

We parted ways, having arranged to meet soon to receive Bojor's call.

* * *

I do not want to be anybody's hero. I do not want to be a dead one! Why should an innocent guy like Meka die because he tried to practice his profession, going to court in defence of innocent peasants?

* * *

When Ovigwe told me that Shata had been picked up, I guessed that they must have pieced information together to get to me. I had to move on or change tactics. So, although I remained on campus, I never slept in my place. Two nights in a row, I crashed into the classrooms when it was very late. I avoided walking in dark places or staying alone in quiet places.

* * *

What has become of Granny, Bojor's father and mother? A security apparatus that arrested the pregnant wife of a journalist in place of her husband wanted for publishing seditious materials could do anything to achieve its objectives. Worried, I faced the black bottle for consolation.

* * *

Tension was high in the land, resulting from high-handed acts by government officials. All the unions were banned to forestall protests and industrial actions. Newspaper houses became more careful as more and more journalists were picked up, tortured and released. The Television Station that played the footage was shut down. However, trouble started from the most unexpected quarters.

It was at the school of Nursing and Midwifery. The Students' Union leader, a rather quiet, easy-going fellow, unusually loved by both the authorities and students had got into a fracas with some policemen. He was mercilessly beaten and hospitalised, with a broken jaw.

Protests started that night, led mainly by female students, who stubbornly refused to listen to their principal. They sacked the school, barricaded the gates and called for a judicial probe into the incident.

'What has Jega done?' became a refrain. It was picked up in different campuses. Policemen were sent to all the tertiary institutions in the federal capital with little success in quelling the protests.

Gradually, the protest spread to other states, taking a new dimension as different interest groups joined in the demonstrations. Each institution identified its peculiar problems and sent its demands to the authorities and then asked the big question: what has Jega done? Before long, it became a call to an end to military rule. From all the campuses, there was a general outcry against dictatorship. Chants followed:

All we are saying,
No more soldiers.

On and on…

I woke up late the next morning, and there was an unusual calm. The usual chanting that had characterised daybreaks was not there. I came out of the room and noticed students in clusters.

'They are one and the same,' a student was saying. At this point I heard the sound of martial music. A voice introduced itself as a member of the Redemption Council and went on to announce a change in the leadership. It closed all borders, called for calm and announced freedom for all political detainees. It promised a full investigation into the death of Barrister Meka.

Later that evening, a smiling General with a funny Indian accent announced himself as the new leader. The Press soon gave him General Ismaila because of the ever-ready smile on his face. He announced some revolutionary measures such as a three-month transition programme to democracy and amnesty for all. He encouraged politicians from political parties and representatives to get ready to take over. The military, he said would be subordinate to civil authority.

The politicians and journalists went up in arms against the government. How could they organise political parties and take over power in three months, they asked.

A government spokesman casually hinted at a Press briefing, after a lot of questions.

'If the politicians cannot take over in three months, the Head of State will continue, probably as a civilian president.

If a blind man falls into a pot of soup
No one would blame him
But if open eyes of a man lead him
Inside the same soup the song would be different

9

Events of the next few days were like a slow motion film. Shata came out of detention, completely deaf in one ear. He had lost his hearing ability to the truncheon of angry interrogators who wanted to know how Bojor got the tapes in faraway Canada. Our first encounter when he came out of the can was a sad one.

the president's mistakes and excesses
have become national policies

A gaunt-looking fellow stood in front of Shata's room, wearing only a singlet and a pair of shorts. Sitting in different positions were people most of whom I had never met before. The gaunt fellow had a smile on his face.
'Brughoro… you must be the tenth wonder.'
'Shata, is this you? What have they done to you?'
'Nothing.'
'Nothing?'
'Nothing, compared with what they did to the others?'
'I'm happy your soul is intact.'
'Don't be too sure.'
'Hum…?'
'I lost something there. Yes I did,' he was saying, smiling bravely. 'The next time I see a revolution coming, I'll go the other way.'
'You must not lose faith because of the scoundrels in power,' I said.
He kept smiling. In the corners of his eyes, there were tears. I embraced him and he responded with emotions and broke down in a heart-rending cry, 'Why? Why?' The visitors started to leave one after

the other. As they left, they looked in my direction, as if their burden had been reduced with my coming. The masses do not want crying heroes perhaps. It was left for me to rehabilitate my friend and ideological brother.

Being a minority should not be a disadvantage
In a democracy

A general feeling of hope came on the land, borne by the face of the smiling General. Mrs Meka was privately settled, after the two men were given life terms. It all baffled me. Two days later, I went to Meka's house. Anne embraced me like old times. There was a new sparkle in her eyes, a sparkle of defiance, defying death and mourning. After the generalities, I blurted out:

'You gave them an easy settlement".

"Bru, come, let's go to my study.'

In the study, away from the ears and eyes of other visitors, I got to know why and how my friend's wife withdrew the suit against the government from court.

'The General himself came visiting.'

'You mean the new…'

'Yes General Ismaila himself. I was so confused. Here he was smiling and promising that the fellows would be brought to book, and my husband would be honoured posthumously. I…'

'You mean General Ismaila entered this house?'

'Yes.'

'Tell me. How did it happen? Who gave him the address?'

'It was in the evening at about 9.30p.m. Most of the sympathizers had gone home. I was getting ready to go to bed when the bell at the gate rang. I sent Ada to see who was at the gate. When she came back, she said a policewoman wanted to speak to me.'

'A policewoman?'

'Yes. I asked her to open the gate and allow her in. I also insisted that Ada must sit in the room if I must talk with her. The policewoman was all jittery. Then she said I had a visitor at the gate who wanted to specially see me and offer his sympathies. I asked why the visitor needed permission to see me and why he must come late at night. To this she calmly said that when I saw the visitor, I would understand. She brought out a phone and spoke into it saying something like 'she is ready to see you now.' Just then, I heard a car start. It drove to the front balcony, and a chubby fellow came down from the car, wearing a white caftan. He looked vaguely familiar. When he entered the house, I recognised him immediately. It was General Ismaila. He gave a broad smile, exposing his gap tooth. He was so humble and kind that I could not match his kind gestures with the dastardly actions once attributed to him. After nearly two hours he convinced me to drop any legal battle. He gave me a cheque for fifteen million naira, which he said should tide me over. 'It is no replacement for your husband. No, this is not. Nothing and nobody can replace your courageous husband. It is not a compensation for the loss. Who can pay for the sharp mind of your late husband and all what he would have given the country had he lived. Let us put all of this behind us and build a new nation. Let your husband's death be one of the sacrifices we had to make for the new nation to emerge.'

'I didn't give an answer on that day because it took me by surprise. Of course I told him how much I appreciated his coming to see me personally, but that considering the gravity of the situation, I had to consult other members of the family and friends. He did not push, nor did he insist I should decide immediately. In fact, he told me stories about how they had tried to undermine the authority of the last government, particularly when state officials started to murder innocent citizens. It was too neat, too pure to be real. I asked for three days, during which time I consulted with my parents and Meka's brothers. They all advised me to take the money and face the future.'

'Just like that?'

'Yes. Just like that.'

I burned inside. Here was a reformer, visiting a widow late in the night to offer a bribe with taxpayers' money. My friend's wife accepted the money in order to save the government from embarrassment.

'But Anne, do you think that Meka would have approved?'

'The circumstances would have been different. Now I don't know.'

'I think that we should have pursued the matter in court as a deterrent to future killers.'

'Bru, you see, one has to count his gains and assess his weaknesses. If they decide to knock me down as they did to Meka, what can anyone of us do? Nothing.'

I thought this over and concluded that perhaps under the circumstance, she took the best decision to safeguard her life and her future. But the cost of sacrificing one's principle was high:

> *not even the silence of the wary one amounted*
> *to anything. If the shop owner leaves his wares for*
> *strangers to meddle with, what right has the wayfarer*
> *to catch thieves of the despoilers?*

'The principle is gone.' I said aloud.

'Yes, in a way. But I've gained something; we've gained something. Meka's death has made a point. The country can never be the same again.'

We discussed all subjects under the sun, just like old times, when Meka would lock himself up in his study and we would go on and on into the wee hours of the morning. She said that the policewoman whom she fondly called Jumai had become her personal friend. Outside official hours, she visits her. I didn't warn her that she was a spy. She would not have believed me. Anne was still at heart the soft daughter of a soft establishment father.

When a smiling shark becomes friendly with a lamb,
Let the mother of the sheep eat knives for defence.

The last thing we said about the new military government was that the Head of State promised freedom to all. Can we have freedom under a military regime?

* * *

I got home very late that night. Anne wanted me to stay over like old times when passionate discussions would keep us till late in the night. I politely declined, offering all kinds of excuses. First, I longed to be alone in my room. The details of her encounter with the smiling general were too much for me. Secondly, though I did not tell her, I thought it was not decent to stay overnight with a widow. I did not want tongues to wag.

As I brought out my key to open my door, the nozzle of a gun appeared from nowhere.

'Stay where you are,' a voice ordered.

'Any false move, you are a goner,' another voice added.

'Armed robbers,' I thought to myself. What did they think they could get from me?

'Put up your hands and turn back slowly.'

I obeyed. Behind me were a dozen men clad in green fatigues. Soldiers! Was this an arrest? In the centre of the semi-circle was a civilian, a tall thin man, with the eyes of a dangerous snake, made bright by the reflections of the light.

'Where is your key?'

I produced it.

'We are going to search your room.'

'What for?' I asked.

From nowhere a slap landed on my face. It must have come from the back, because it blasted my eardrum. I staggered to one side.

'Don't ask stupid questions.'

I was handcuffed and taken inside the house. Two men ransacked my room, taking each item methodically.

Finally they announced their verdict: 'we can't find it.'

I then ventured.

'If you tell me what you are looking for, I just might help you.'

Nobody appeared to listen. With a flick of his fingers, Snake Eyes dismissed his minions:

'Where is the master tape?'

'Master tape?'

'Yes, Brughoro, tell us where the master tape is.'

Here was a complete stranger calling my name so familiarly.

'I don't know what you are talking about.'

'Don't play hard to get. My boys there are itching for action. Don't be carried away by the sweet nonsense you hear on radio and television. State security remains primary to us.'

He paused and lit a cigarette, blowing the smoke into my face. I felt something was flowing over my shoulder. Blood was dripping from my ear.

'See what your boys have done to my ear.'

'You'll get more of that if you don't co-operate. Where is the master tape which the Barrister gave to you?'

'He did not give it to me. He kept it somewhere. I don't know where. We both agreed that I should not know.'

'Why?'

'Just in case a situation like this arose.'

'Where is your copy?'

'I don't have a copy.'

'You are lying.'

'No I'm not. My copy was given to my friend before he left for Canada.'

Abruptly, he turned and went outside.

Two soldiers came and pushed me out. From their windows, my neighbours were peeping. I then screamed out loud.

'Neighbours, soldiers are taking me away. Please contact Mrs Meka, my late friend's wife.'

A blow landed on my head and I passed out.

When I came to, I was lying on the floor inside a room, an empty room. Although the room was hot, the ground was cold. Gradually, the nightmare returned in full force. The door opened, and somebody poked his head inside:

'He's still on the other side.'

'How do you know?'

'His eyes are shut. He is still lying in the position he was when we last came in.'

'Go get water! I no want any Pressman to come die for my neck here. Where is the bastard Olugbode? I told him to take it easy. He refused. The fellow does not look like a person who can take a good beating.'

I didn't want water poured on me, so I moved to my right side, and sat up, rubbing my hands on my face.

'You had a long sleep.'

I did not answer.

'You've been sleeping since yesterday evening.'

'What time is it?' I managed to ask. My lips felt heavy.

'7 p.m. Now get up, you are going to eat and continue your interrogation.'

'I'm not hungry.'

Roughly he pulled me up. My legs felt wooden. My head ached. We entered a long corridor. He asked me to go right. I shuffled on till he ordered me to enter a room.

I opened the door. In a time like this, the pain of torture is aided by the feeling of anything-can-happen, from incapacitation to death.

Inside the room was a man sitting behind a desk. He was busy writing, and did not raise his head when we entered.

'We are here?'

'Any progress?' he asked still not raising his head.

'None. I'm about to start. Sit down here!' he ordered me. I gladly crumbled into a sofa.

'Are you ready to tell us where the tape is?'

'I don't know where it is. If I knew it, I would tell you. After all, a copy is already abroad, why should I still conceal the master tape at the risk of my life.'

The writing man then looked up. He had the face of an old monkey, with all the whiskers and wrinkles in place.

'So you sent a tape to foreign enemies? You can be charged for treason.'

I said nothing. There was a nothing to say to the fool.

'Give us details. How did the tape get there?'

There was a loud knock, followed by a shoving sound, which forced the door open. A fat man waddled in, looking angry and ready for a fight.

'Where is the man who is bringing all this trouble?'

'Look at him here,' monkey-face said, pointing at me and springing to attention at the same time.

'This man is pure trouble, you hear me? Set him free. Let him go with his trouble. I have received four phone calls from headquarters in the last one hour. I didn't know that it was a mosquito like this that was disturbing my peace.'

'Stand up at once,' he roared. 'Stay out of trouble. Just remember that godfathers are not always around.'

He stormed out and I walked into freedom.

Outside at the gate, a car horn hooted and I looked in its direction. I stopped moving, trying to be sure of what the situation was like before taking any action.

'Bru, it's me. Come here!'

I dragged myself to the car and we zoomed off.

'Thanks for coming for me,' I said.

'It's nothing. You are alive, and that is something. If they had taken your life, what could I have done?'

Suddenly, I was overwhelmed with emotions.

'I appreciate your coming for me in spite of the risk.'

'Don't mention. Our struggle is collective, and that is our strength. The focus will now change, because our real problems back at home have not changed.'

'The killings and arrests are meant to distract us.'

* * *

After I was arrested, all the tenants in my compound had a meeting. It was agreed that a delegation should go to Mrs Meka. The next morning, two elderly men went to see Anne. When they arrived in the house, Jumai was chatting with Anne. After the two men identified themselves, they told their story.

'Can you describe any of the men?'

They tried to give a description.

'Which kind of vehicle?'

'Two Peugeot 504 cars, station wagon.'

'I took down the number of one of the cars.'

'Good,' Jumai said. She noted down the number and asked them to leave. Anne thanked them, offering them drinks which they politely rejected. They went to Shata's place. He was lying on the floor in his room. After greetings, they told him what happened.

'Soldiers?'

'Yes.'

'You're sure?'

'Yes we saw them.'

'I'm not going there for the rest of my life. I'm not going near any soldier.'

Jumai made some calls, both to the headquarters and local offices. She left the house promising to make enquiries and to call back. At about 6 p.m., she called to say that Anne would receive a message soon from the Military Intelligence.

'General Ismaila himself ordered your release.'

There was nothing to say.

Even killers can save us sometimes

* * *

Co-tenants received me back, sharing in the joy and thanking Mrs. Meka for acting very fast. The oldest man in the compound invited everyone to his flat. Drinks appeared. He cleared his throat and said:

'We all come from different ethnic groups. But we are one. I have no quarrel with you. You have none with me. If we quarrel, we can always settle our differences.'

'We are our brother's keepers. Your problems are mine, and mine are yours. If we continue to live like this there will be peace.'

'See Mrs. Meka who has just lost her husband. She still helped to rescue another man.'

'May her days be long!'

'*Ise!*' we chorused.

'May she have the strength to cut her yam and eat it!

'*Ise!*'

'May the killers of her husband be caught and punished!'

'*Ise!*'

'May her children grow up to be men and women of honour.'

'*Ise!*'

'They will outshine their fathers.'

'*Ise!*

'Somebody seized their father's paddle mid-stream. May no one go near the children and succeed.'

'*Ise!*'

'And may those who deny us peace never know peace, in the name of God Almighty.'

'Ise!'

Drinks were served. An hour later Anne drove home having obtained a promise that I must see the doctor.

* * *

The doctor prescribed bed rest for me. He examined my ear and said that there was no real injury. The lobe got torn as a result of 'violent impact.' He wanted me to stay in the hospital, but I said no. First, I had no money for any big hospital bills, and I did not want to see myself as an invalid. I preferred to rest at home.

In the evening, Ovigwe came to see me, in the company of Shata. I was surprised.

'Ovigwe, how now?'

'Fine. Sorry about it all. I hope the bastards did not injure you?'

'No just minor bruises.'

'Sorry,' Shata said.

'You abandoned me, Shata, you abandoned me in my hour of trial,' I said.

'How?' Ovigwe asked.

'My co-tenants went to tell him, and he said he couldn't come because he did not want anything with soldiers.'

'Is it true?' Ovigwe asked him.

'Yes, it's true. You see, I don't know how to explain it.'

'Try, try harder.'

'I have this phobia. I don't know whether it has anything to do with the treatment which they gave me there. You see I get physically and critically nervous anytime I encounter security. Even in print 'security' makes me tremble. I react. So you understand me?'

I kept silent. Ovigwe smiled.

'Aren't you exaggerating?' she asked.

'You see, that's why I didn't want to tell you initially. I know myself. I know that I'm not yet what I used to be. I tremble physically.'

'You should see a psychiatrist,' I said.

'Bru, it has not reached that stage,' Ovigwe countered laughingly.

'Yes it has. It has reached the stage. In fact I've already seen one.'

'You have?' I asked sitting up.

'Yes.'

'What did he say to you?'

'He talked to me for hours, gave me some drugs to control my nerves and relax my mind. He said something like anxiety neurosis, one of the symptoms of depression.'

'They did you in brother, they did you in,' I said. 'But you must not let them kill your spirit. Once they do that, we are all gone.'

'It's hard, Bru, it's hard. But I'll try. I need your support. I need to stay around people whose social antennae are on the same wavelength as mine. I need to talk, avoid any distractions for sometime, and later confront all my fears headlong. I know that I should not be afraid. But I'm afraid. I need a kind of pilgrimage into myself, and I'll be washed anew.'

There was silence for a while. Shata's long speech had sobered me a little, and in a way, we had been driven into examining ourselves critically, re-assessing ourselves, seeing our woes and the pains we had to live with. All over the country, there was a feeling of want, and the word 'stress' became too familiar in the minds of children. Yet we had to live. Ovigwe tried to cheer us up.

'The new man has promised to improve relations with the citizenry. He's freed political prisoners. That gives some hope.'

'Some hope indeed,' Shata sneered.

'You don't believe him?'

'Believe him? Drop that word when you are dealing with our nation's soldiers. Believe a brute whose sole objective is to obtain power? Don't be naïve, Ovigwe!'

I said nothing.

'Bru, say something! After all, the present regime is better than the last one,' Ovigwe said.

'How?' I asked.

'He has promised a return to civil rule. He has also set political prisoners free.'

'And thrown new ones into the can.'

'Such as ...'

'Me. Yes... It's the same regime which promised everyone freedom that threw me into the can, after being thoroughly beaten.'

'It's an error, isn't it?' Ovigwe cried. 'When senior officers got the report, you were freed.'

'Senior officers, my foot! The Head of State himself ordered my release.'

'You don't mean that, do you?' Shata asked.

'Every word of it! The smiling General has a lot to do.'

'You are a big shot, aren't you?'

165

'I'm not. I'm just lucky. How many people in this country have access to a phone, not to talk of calling a General who is the Head of State? If it can happen to me, just imagine what the ordinary people suffer.'

'He has to get rid of all fifth columnists within the government,' Shata said.

'That's not the solution. I think you are simplifying the issue. The Army itself is a fifth columnist in our Federation. The officers are always ready to cash in on the failures of politicians. Are they any better?'

'In what sense do you mean?' Shata asked.

'In terms of administration, progress, planning the economy, stamping out corruption.'

'Have you been living in this country? In the past, the Army succeeded in giving that impression. It's all changed now. On the average, officers are now as corrupt as politicians.'

'You have a point there,' Shata said, 'but don't you think we need the Army now to guarantee stability?'

'That's wishful thinking. By its training, an Army keeps itself off politics. It insulates itself from the hustle and bustle of civilian life, because civilian life is not regimented. For our Army to keep its own idea of order, it must use force, because force keeps it in order. Extending force to the civil populace is a way of brutalizing people.'

'You are so pessimistic about the Army.' Ovigwe cut in, 'Have we not had Military leaders who transformed their countries?'

'Count them?'

'I can't do so easily,' he replied, 'but in Ghana, the Army handed over power to the civilians after restoring order.'

'What did you say? Handed over power after restoring order. Not building the economy. As long as the army keeps interfering, we shall not witness any real growth.'

'I agree with you Bru,' Shata said, 'the Army seems to keep a semblance of order. Underneath the concept of order, there is rottenness and decadence. I think politicians should learn how to control their affairs, using their political charms.'

'Not charms,' I said, 'they should carry the people along. No idea is sacrosanct. The whole idea of representation is that once a decision is taken, once you are represented by a man or woman popularly elected, one is bound by their decisions. Unpopular decisions cannot see the light of day. Even if they are taken, citizens witness the debate and ultimately concede victory to the majority.'

'It doesn't work out so neatly as you put it,' Shata said, 'what you are saying is the ideal.'

'Yes it is an ideal, but we can strive towards it.'

At this point there was a knock at the door and Anne came in. Within a short time, she seemed to have overcome her grief. Although she was not flashily dressed, she did not look as dull as she did in the last few weeks. When I commented, she said something like 'Meka (God bless him) would never have wanted me to go about looking a mummy on his account. My sorrow is in my heart, and I know I'll bear it until my dying day.'

After this I never commented on her looks anymore.

She said she just came to check on me, and to see how this bachelor boy was coping in the aftermath of the encounter with the soldiers. Shata was unusually silent, eyeing her from a distance. When Anne commented on Shata's withdrawal, I said a bit lightly:

'He is suffering from post-assault syndrome, PAS'

'So sorry Shata, take heart. After all you are alive aren't you? Cheer up.'

As if by magic, Shata livened up a bit again till Anne left. I commented on it and he replied:

'It would have been beastly of me to remain gloomy after a woman who just lost her husband, my friend had reminded me that I was still alive, while her husband was gone. It got to me.'

We all saw her off to her car, parked on the road. On the way back to the house, Ovigwe remembered that Bojor had sent some photographs to her the week before. She produced them from her handbag and gave me a letter, addressed to me. I put it aside, waiting till I was all alone to read its contents.

The photographs showed Bojor in different places of activity. One was a poetry reading session. He was the black face in a sea of white faces. In another, he was at a symposium, seated at the far right of the moderator. I didn't recognise him in the third photograph, because he had grown a beard, and had added some weight to his small stature, thanks to the quality of food he was eating (as he had confirmed to me in an earlier letter). He had the crucifix on in one, in which he posed with an old white lady who looked like withered matter ready for the grave.

'My friend has grown a beard,' I said, staring at the photograph, 'he looks like a real revolutionary.'

'I think he should be careful,' Ovigwe said cautiously, 'I've written to him to take it easy.'

'You, you mean you have already…'

'Bru, I've never told you. I always have nightmares with Bojor always at the centre. A particular image comes to me every night.'

She broke down. I had thought Ovigwe was too strong to break down like this. This soft side took me unawares.

'Easy Ovigwe, easy. Nothing bad is going to happen.'

'Tell me about your dreams.' Shata said.

'Sometimes I see him walking into the hills, all alone. When I call, he never looks back. Always forward looking. At other times I see him inside a ship, his back turned to me.'

I broke into a loud laugh, trying to break the tension. Shata was not amused. He seemed to have taken it all seriously.

'You've got to pray hard,' Shata was saying, 'pray very hard.'

'Don't tell me you have taken the dreams of a woman who thinks she is going to lose her husband seriously! Don't be superstitious, the revolution will go astray.'

'Beware of the man who is not superstitious. How is it said? A man without superstition has no spirit.'

Ovigwe was silent in tears, her big eyeballs rolled in their sockets, looking red.

'Ovigwe be strong. As long as we think positively, nothing bad can really happen to him.'

'Yes I know. But in his last letter, he talked about being followed everywhere.'

'Followed?' both of us echoed.

'Who by?'

'Two white men.'

'They must be racist.'

'He must not move alone.'

Later, much later, we saw Ovigwe off.

When we got back to room, Shata looked pensive.

'Bru, the situation is bad. I see the image in my dream. We've got to pray hard. '

'You mean the same…'

'Yes, the same dream! I think we are being given a signal.'

'I don't understand all this.' I said, remembering the dream I had on the night when Bojor came to tell me about the scholarship.

'Is there anybody in his village we can consult?' I heard Shata asking. Granny came to my mind. 'He must remember to look back,' was all that came to my lips.

'Remember to do what?'

'To look back,' I answered.

'That's a poem.'

'No. It's what Granny said to me the last time we visited his hometown together.'

'Don't you think we should go to the village and…'

'… and tell them that tragedy is about to befall their family?'

We left it at that.

* * *

Later, left alone in the harsh coldness of my room, I remembered all the dreams, our dreams with intense emotions. Granny's words came echoing. Uncle's too. I tossed about in bed, unable to sleep. I tuned the radio. BBC was reading out its tales of disaster all around the world in form of news. I switched it off.

I got up from the bed, and picked up my Bible. An envelope fell. I picked it up. It was Bojor's letter to me, handed over by Ovigwe, earlier on in on evening. I went back to bed, laid on my back and read Bojor's letter or poem:

12th of February
Dear Bru,
    i shall go into the alcove of my dreams
a virgin with the feet of an old maiden
my pen shall be testimony
even if some creep behind me daily
recording the experiences of the poet
in the climate of the snow
my friends, yes friends
shall bear the remnants of the sacrifice
which scholarship bestowed on the vagrant
poet sojourning away from the lizard
eyes of uniformed men.
Meka rest in peace
and we live in pieces attempting
to join fragments of existence
together as we trudge on in
the valley of decisions
remember 'come to my keyhole'
i remember and it is like yesterday
though the embers have since
metamorphosed into tongues of fire
shadows

shadows every where i go
and i tremble because you are not here
to comfort me as in the lagoon front
i see granny's eye's winking
at me and beckoning me
to return home
and save the chicken from being
sacrificed before its time
Anne?
Shata?
Opuda?
ask them to write
they must write and build bridges
across the mighty seas
i hear the General is near the
throne
his chest heaving
a whip in his hand
a smile in his mouth
and fire in his tongue
we must not let the sweet
breeze of the rat lull us into
a fatal lethargy
i am spent
                Bru,
                i am spent
it's a cold night
and i miss the warm continent
of my forebears
who laid my eggs in the land
of brotherly warmth far away
from the cold beauty of the
fantastic west
do not tremble
yesterday my nine month stay gave birth
to a three-year stint
my mind they say is too fertile to be left
at the door of an M.A.
i must take a doctorate
but i still see you in my dreams
and remember Opuda of lagoon front
i remember Anne
and i know i must return

to drink the milk of the black
continent
soon brother soon
when i return what will you be like
will you see me naked as i am
                as I used to be
                will you read my poetry upside
down as white faces do here
will you say my content is
now white
and capsize the calabash of my
inspiration
what will it be like?
what will it be like?
console Ovigwe as it was
in the beginning
tell her to recreate her dreams
and stand above the splashing
sea which frightens one
tell her her fears
strengthen me and once again
i shall hold my hammer
and caress the anvil perpetually
in joy and beauty

if my dreams fail to emerge
from the depths of the ocean
you must hold the light
in search of that which
i missed as i joined
the
train
of
strangers

        Bojor

P/s   even if water flows
    into the soup pot
    we can still eat it

    granny says we must
    steam it until

the stranger dries out
aluta!

I read the poem three times that night, savouring its beauty and pondering over the layers of meaning embedded in his lines. I concentrated on the lines which reinforced my conviction that he would return peacefully, I read the line:

and I know I must return
to drink the milk of the black continent.

I fell asleep.

* * *

I woke up next morning feeling groggy. It was a dreamless sleep and I soon forgot all my fears. I got into a tune, a cheerful one. It was a tune, which came from the subconscious, a song my father used to sing rather solemnly in my boyhood days. The words were something like this:

Jesus knows all about our struggles
He will help when danger is near
There's not a friend like the lowly Jesus
No not one, no not one

The rest of the words were lost in my memory of time. I remember my mother told me that anytime my father sang this song, it was a sure sign that he was broke. And because he was always broke, the song became very familiar in the house.

After a bath and a cup of tea, I headed for the bus stop, en route to my office. All the passengers were rather solemn, and for a minute, I wondered whether there was a national tragedy which I had missed.

I got off the weird bus and walked the short distance to my office. When I got to the other side of the road, a Volkswagen Beetle car parked in front of me, and somebody was beckoning me excitedly. I looked at him. It was my lecturer at the French school, where Bojor and I took a diploma two years back.

'You hear say Bojor don die?'

'What?' I asked, cold fear in my chest.

'His body was brought home on Friday and buried.'

'No, no…No…!'

'Come to my office for details.' I raised my head and saw a small crowd in front of the office. French teacher had sped off. I walked across the road to Ovigwe, not knowing what to say.

'You hear say Bojor don die?'

10

And the grey message came, neatly covered in a grey envelop. The world became a different place, a grey place as a total stranger narrated to me how the bowl of life was taken from the man sojourner who was admonished to always look back. It was a shallow dream, bitter and seamy as Granny's voice came re-echoing in my afternoon dream. The dream, so feared, so distant had come lurking into the life of the wary poet, and the news came in a casual manner.

You hear say Bojor don die?

The curses from my heart could have shaken the foundations of Babylon.

Dis no be breaking news...

Dear Mr. Brughoro,

There are times when circumstances force people to face a common fate, foe or destiny. By way of introduction, I am Rev. Cornelius Obiajulu, a Priest pursuing my Doctorate in Toronto. I am writing this letter to you to help myself and to acquaint you with the beauty that was our friend's life while he lived here. He always spoke of you, and highly too, fondly recalling your influence in his life. So when he finally left us, I felt that I must communicate with someone from the other side, someone I could talk to and purge myself of the intense pain gnawing my insides.

Bojor's death in spite of myself shook my faith in the justness of universal law and order. For sometime, I questioned the very reason for living, asking: why? all the time even when on official duty as officiating Priest for African Catholics here in Toronto. The core of my doubt was this: why should Providence allow a man so blessed with innate intelligence as to be a genius to die before his time?

Bojor Aruedon came to us here in December, last year, full of life and zest, taking everybody by storm. His diminutive stature tempted one to ignore him. My first encounter with him was at a symposium organised by African Heritage Foundation. He sat at the back of the auditorium quietly listening to the debate on whether or not African countries should be forgiven their debts. I never noticed him till it was questions and comments time. In fact, at the time he made his contributions, the moderator was getting ready to round off discussions.

At the back of the hall, one arm shot into the air somewhat diffidently, and with some reluctance the moderator allowed him to speak. With disarming casualness, he spoke about the plight of African countries and the reign of illiterate tyrants who incur debt on behalf of unfortunate citizens, hapless and helpless in the face of a terrible machinery of oppression. I still remember his words because they were extensively quoted the next day in the daily papers:

'The debt burden is indeed one of the effects of misrule in the African continent. Men, trained to defend the sovereignty of their nations suddenly became power holders in the guise of redeemers. But because they were not trained to do long term administrative and political planning, they tended to take measures which were at best palliatives in the face of mounting crises.'

The tone and manner of his presentation were indeed sobering.

Of course, one of his strengths was his eloquence and articulation, often times sounding as if he was reading from a book. But the content of his mind was staggering to say the least.

He formed the African Poetry Club, drawing poets from America and the West Indies. All this he did within two

175

months of his arrival in the country. The African Poetry Club became a rallying point for all Africans, who wanted to know about their home continent.

He was also a member of the Pan-African Movement, a group that provided him the forum to launch his historical attack on the dictatorship in our dear native land. He got the support of most activists in the City.

When General Maliki was toppled, he became a hero in the eyes of the local people here.

Early in the year, he visited the US where he presented his poetry in colleges, receiving standing ovations in all his presentations. At the end of the tour, a publisher accepted two volumes of his poetry manuscripts. We hope that Mr. Hopeman will go ahead and publish the collections in the memory of our late friend.

It's so sad referring to Bojor as late, whenever I remember the dynamism of his personality. Late? Why late?

His death was unexpected. There was no warning. One moment he was alive, the next moment he was a corpse. Precisely, he died on 15th February. On the 14th he had attended a Valentine party hosted by a patroness of the Arts in the university. Professor Barbara Brown hosted a party in the common room of the Faculty of Arts. One of the guests at the party was a man, one Mr. Sam Shehu from the Embassy; at least he introduced himself as a staff of the Embassy. He and Bojor got talking for a long while. Bojor performed three of his poems, and as usual the hall exploded in applause. Politely, he acknowledged the ovation and went to a corner to chat up an up-coming poet. Towards midnight, I wanted to discuss our next outing, so I went searching for him. I was told that he had complained about chest pains and had gone home.

'He should take a rest.'

'He needs it.'

'I'll take him to a farm next weekend.'

All friends! These were words to help a friend. The party ended at about three in the morning and I staggered to my room, half drunk with sleepiness.

The next morning, there was a news flash in the campus magazine:

AFRICAN POET DIES OF CARDIAC ARREST

I didn't bother to read the details. I raced to the city morgue to confirm the story. Unfortunately, I was shown the body of my friend lying stone dead in one of the chambers of an indifferent morgue.

Dis na disaster

It was later I got details from Barbara Turner, the Caribbean lady Bojor had been intimate with. Her version was garbled but there was no doubt that our friend had been poisoned. She disclosed that Bojor was restless, after he returned from the party. When she suggested that they should go to a hospital, he refused, saying that he would be alright. He attributed the discomfort to the cold weather, and the stress of the last hectic days. He said the cold weather always chilled his insides.

Barbara prepared a cup of warm beverage for him, which he took. Minutes later, he started coughing terribly and his breathing changed. He started saying things about the last glass of wine which he took at the party, during his discussions with Mr. Sam Shehu. He said something about checking the cup. Alarmed, Barbara called emergency and in minutes an ambulance was wailing at the entrance. Inside the ambulance, he was given respiratory aid. His condition stabilized briefly. At about 3 a.m., he had a massive attack, leading to Cardiac arrest.

So Bojor died.

We suspect that Bojor was murdered because when we contacted the Embassy, we were told that there was nobody that bore the name Sam Shehu on the staff.

Bojor was given poetic, heroic rites of passage. His poems were published in all the local papers including the most extreme pro-white papers. I conducted the service that was done in the Student's Union building. I have enclosed a copy of the funeral oration, which I gave in this letter.

Bojor always spoke of you as a brother and as a friend, a person I could entrust with my life. So I am taking you as the executor of his will, an unwritten will. Make sure that you publish his poems in a collection.

I wish you well. Please do not fail the dead. Honour his memory and I am sure Bojor will rest in peace with the knowledge that his voice has been projected into the future.

I trust you also to console Ovigwe whom Bojor also captured in the last collection of poems he wrote.
It is his only link with the future.

So long,

Reverend B.

I finished reading the letter. The room, even the outside world was silent, waiting for me to make the next move, the clock of the world continued to tick in spite of the cardiac arrest. My mind was inert. I then reached for a copy of the oration read by Rev. B. at my friend's funeral. It read:

At times like this, we are tempted to question all the fine notions of fairness and equity of Providence; we are tempted to query the very basis of human existence and the degree to which we can say that the forces of good are in control of the world, that divine providence caters for all. We are tempted to question the place of a man in the cosmos in relation to fulfilling a mission. We are forced to question death as a blind foe who attacks both the good and the bad with equal brutality and with no sense of logic. We are tempted to ask why could the Almighty imbue a man with so much intellect and ability and let him die even before the world sees the hand of God in his life. In fact, we might be tempted to blaspheme.

As for me, I have not come to terms with Bojor's death, and its implications for humanity. Why is it that I am not the one lying stone dead in that casket, and a man of genius explaining to the world that a loss of man of modest intelligence is insignificant to the dynamism of the world? I am sure all of us here are silently asking these questions in our hearts, attempting to see the WHY in the puzzle that is Bojor's death.

At such times, we return to Scriptures which provide answers to all questions. God is Right and Just and will never allow the order of things to degenerate. So we are commanded to submit ourselves to Divine Will, not questioning, to be obedient like Abraham. The intellectual St. Paul says:

Nay but, O man, who art thou that repliest against God?
Shall the thing formed say to him that formed it, why hast
Thou made thus?
Hath not the potter power over the clay of the same lump
to make one vessel unto honour, and another unto
dishonour?

What we can infer is that The Almighty has a purpose for the creation of any man. Perhaps his purpose in Bojor has been fulfilled by the way he enriched our lives, the way he shone in the last months of his sojourn on earth.

At the theological level, I have accepted Bojor's death as an act allowed by the Almighty to remind us about the frailty of mortal man. The core of my acceptance of this loss is faith in the omnipotence of the Almighty, His Absolute control over all the Elements of Nature and Spirit. When I detach myself from the essence of his faith, Bojor's death becomes an error in the equation of creation. Yet we know that there is no error in creation. The truth is that as humans we never know how positives and negatives of the cosmos balance themselves out. At the infinite level, much higher than we can see or comprehend, Bojor's loss is a gain to the universe.

It is difficult for those who were close to him to accept such an explanation without a blind faith. How can his father or his young mother or his young fiancé accept such an explanation, knowing that the physical intimacy is gone? How can the fiancé for instance accept the explanation that her love dreams are all dreams? It is difficult, but the only way we can continue to have faith in the Almighty, the only way we can continue to live is by believing that, there is a Right somewhere, which we have not comprehended.

As we all know, Bojor came from Africa barely seven months ago. To some of us blacks here, who had never visited the continent, he was the Black Stone and he became the link with the future. He came with a vitality of his own, and added a spirituality which we all benefited from. Often times, I met black young undergraduates, in his room, where he tried to explain the last continent to them. Some even came with their mothers.

At this point, a mother in the audience burst into tears, immediately joined by his daughter. Soon the wailing became uncontrollable. It took some five minutes to restore calm.

This is the extent to which his life enriched ours. This is the extent to which we must remember him. This is the extent to which we must emulate him. This is the extent to which we must transfer his virtues to posterity.

Nobody knows his time. As we are today, so was he; as he is, so shall we be some day. Scriptures says:

for the living know that they shall die:
but the dead know not anything,
neither have they any more a portion
forever in any thing that is done under
the sun.
whatsoever thy had findeth to do,
do it with thy might, for there is no work,
nor device, nor knowledge, nor wisdom,
in the grave, whither thou goest.
Eccle.9: 5-10

With these words let us comfort one another.

I came to the end of the letter and the end of a phase of the struggle. Bojor's death brought me face to face with the reality of the power of the State to wipe one out of the cosmos at any time, without warning. Distance was no barrier to the bloodthirsty soldiers who held the land to ransom. Until Bojor, one had always associated death with people in distant places. In my subconscious, Bojor was meant to live forever.

We arrived in Orereame, two days after we received news about his death. Ovigwe and I left Lagos with some hope, feeling that Bojor might be alive, and that we would see him again just emerging from the dressing room or from backstage after playing a role. But the small mound of earth at the back of Bojor's father's house destroyed the final illusion.

'He was buried there.' said a youth appointed to take us to the grave, not pointing fingers. He jutted out this chin and indicated an unmarked grave for one of the greatest minds that ever lived.

'You know, he wasn't married, he didn't have a child, his parents are still alive. No elaborate burial rites for a man who died before his time. Youths must not be in a hurry to die.'

His exit did not hit the radio's eardrum.

* * *

We had nothing to say. Ovigwe kept muffled sounds from her throat, dabbing her eyes occasionally.

'As soon as the body arrived,' the young man was saying, 'his age mates were invited to open the coffin and confirm that it was indeed Bojor's body. Within an hour, the grave was ready. Only his age mates buried him. His father did not even come out of the house.'

'But why?'

No one answered Ovigwe. I was not sure whether she was asking why Bojor was buried without a ceremony or why he died.

We shall pour the proper dust over your body;
We shall return to give you a martyr's burial.

Later that evening, we went to see Granny. She recognised my voice immediately.

She had aged, terribly, looking withered and withdrawn, without any life in her voice.

'They beat me up and killed my son,' was all she said.

We sat in the room, no one saying anything, too busy with our own thoughts.

Before we left, Granny offered a prayer and concluded:

'May we never answer the night call in the morning of our lives.'

'*Ise*!' we answered.

Back in my house, Anne had left a note for me:

Fate can be cruel. Within two months, you've lost two friends. I pray God to give you the spirit, to give you the zeal to continue and believe in the boundless possibilities of the human life.

For me, it is a single blow, whereas for you, it's two. You must continue to be yourself.

I tossed the note somewhere and slept for twenty-four hours.

Let the dragons of hell drag me to the portals of death and shout the genius of the night. The night call must not be answered in the morning of one's life.

Ovigwe became my companion, and I her companion. Our grief brought us together. Bojor was our regular topic. We both x-rayed his life and wondered what it was worth?

'Unfair, it's unfair,' became an familiar refrain from the lips of Ovigwe, and I had nothing tangible to mend the heart of a young woman brutalised by the sudden demise of a lover, a first and only lover. Before my eyes, she dried up, losing flesh and gloss by the day. Her zest diminished, and often I caught her talking to herself. I then knew that something had to be done.

She felt really bad about not being informed that her fiancй died, and received a shoddy burial because he did not marry and have kids like a real man. He was a national hero who deserved a heroic burial. She was right. A month later, we gave a proper burial to Bojor in the full glare of the media. All our friends came, including some funny looking fellows we suspected came from Security. One evening, I sat Ovigwe down, and told her why Bojor must be put behind her. I was tactful, stressing the positive.

'I spoke to Voice Publishers yesterday, they are willing to publish Bojor's poems.'

She cheered up suddenly.

'O… that will be beautiful! I hope the terms are favourable?'

'Yes. They asked for a sum that could aid the production.'

'But his works are good. I think they can publish it themselves. Why do we need to pay?'

One Bojor is gone. They expect us to do the publishing and public relations. I don't mind that as long as the work gets eventually published. Once people read him, the other manuscripts will be hunted for.'

We both threw ourselves into collating some of his poems. It was a tiring work, though we were buoyed by the belief and conviction that we were doing something for a dead friend. Echoes from the past came hitting my ears.

When I'm dead and gone, is that how you will interpret my poems

And Ovigwe's quiet presence brought me back to the present.

'Do you think we should try other publishers?'

'No, VOICE seems to be sincere,' I replied. 'Perhaps after the first, we shall be able to judge.'

Black Souls for Sale came out six months later, and we killed the world with our outpourings of joy. Since Bojor was already known in the media, the reporters and Art Editors were very cooperative. The reviews made our lives better.

We entered the collection in the annual Poetry Competition organised by the National Arts Commission. While we were awaiting a response, we both paid a visit to Anne.

* * *

Anne. We all drifted apart slowly, though anytime we met, the old fire of friendship returned. Sometimes, Shata would be there and we would discuss all matters except the death of our friends. Anne also never let it known that the advance fee given to the publisher came from her. I admired her for that. We were all seated on the stage of life, playing different roles.

even if they return, they will not recognise this act of kindness; brothers till the soil and sisters eat the yam.

When Ovigwe and I arrived at Anne's place one evening, after the usual greetings, she blurted out:
'I think both of you should get married.'
Silence, as she flashed a mischievous, radiant smile. Consciously I had never given a thought to starting a relationship with Ovigwe. I looked at her, and she could not meet my eyes. Was there something I was missing? The silence was odd, broken by Anne's laughter and:
'You look very cute together and I suppose our dear lost ones would not mind if we recycled love amongst ourselves. After all, life must continue.'
'Life must continue,' I said, 'but one has to get ready for certain things.'
'Snap out of misery, Bru! Bojor and Meka are gone. Ovigwe is still young. I know you are responsible and you are simply concerned with gallantry, taking care of a late friend's woman. But for what? For another man? A stranger who may not appreciate the sacrifices which we have all made?'
Ovigwe sat still, staring at the floor, at one spot. Was there a missing code?
'If those who were dead were to speak, they would tell us to live on. I am sure none of them would encourage us to sacrifice our joys because of their deaths. They died for a cause and as long as we believe in and fight the cause, we would be perpetuating their memories. Let your involvement with Oil People's Movement be the candlelight, your connection with the future.'

I thought about this for a while, imagining what Meka, Bojor, and uncle would say about sacrifice. My own flame had found new outlets, and I stood all alone on the grassland, the oil field of romance, till now. I drifted away, face to face with Meka, with Bojor, with Uncle Odiete.

Postscript

Far, far away in the misty horizon, the crystal nature of pure things started a gradual descent into the land of the weary ones, the ones who had fought the colour green to a standstill, resplendent in an array of colours. The colours came from the moon just as their claims came from far above. Everybody knew what had been done, what had been left to the ashes of time, what had been destroyed, and what had to be re-built from the remnants of the encounter. They came to say that they could identify the cause of the hesitations, the cause of the foot-dragging that left everyone gaping. Time cannot stand still and wait for us to catch up with the deep things. But why did we stand aside while they plundered our inheritance, giving us crumbs in the name of oneness? We do not want to blame our history, but our representatives tell us to wait till the appointed time. When is the appointed time?

Time! In time, the new cycle began and a merry-go-round feast, presided over by scoundrels started. Of course, its pain was different, benign, and almost acceptable. Yet the ground records remained the same. Time has not changed it. Even in time, there are still flares as the forces of power shell the land with burning flames, destroying vegetation, depleting the ozone, truncating lives.

Inside the inferno, the old, the weak, the infirm, the strong all squirm, waiting for the thunder of sacrifice to lift them out of the hell which the men of power had created. And the men of power laugh on, sucking the dark gold with their Dracula teeth. Always in flowing robes, they scorn the fishermen, owners of the land whose God gave them the liquid to own, fight for and preserve. So whatever the sojourners say, the gift shall return to the legitimate owners. The blood of martyrs will ensure this no matter what they claim and what they do.

Like Bojor's major character in *Rooms and Rivers*, Bojor shall live again. Bojor did not die, will never die. For deep inside all of us, witnesses to the crimes, participants in the spectacle, a new flame has been lit that will burn perpetually even when they crush our bodies with their boots. Because of their elephant size, the beetle is in danger, but the beetle soon learns how to live with tigers, with leopards, with rodents and other animals that threaten its existence. In the quest for survival even weaklings soon find channels of overcoming physically stronger predators.

Perpetual light will come through the dark death of the patriot. It was not a going that we yearned for, nor was it a leave-taking that called for a feast; yet, its droppings must change the direction of the wind, light up the channels.

If they do not follow the lighted path, our tragedy will bomb their conscience till eternity. It may be a forlorn hope, this belief in the ultimate triumph of that which is right in a land where the meeting point between truth and untruth is defined in untruthful terms. Yet it is in our only hope to kill the vampires. Their blood shall water the revolution in fulfilment of Granny's curse.

Even the Pope will feel this one.